ANNIE'S ATTIC MYSTERIES®

The Cats & the Riddle

Jan Fields

Annie's®
AnniesFiction.com

Library of Congress-in-Publication Data
The Cats & the Riddle / by Jan Fields
p. cm.
I. Title
                        2012917582

AnniesFiction.com
800-282-6643
Annie's Attic Mysteries®
Series Editors: Janice Tate and Ken Tate
Series Creator: Stenhouse & Associates, Ridgefield, Connecticut

10 11 12 13 14 | Printed in China | 9 8 7 6

~ 1 ~

The small silver bell hanging over the door of A Stitch in Time tinkled cheerfully as Annie Dawson walked into the needlecraft store. Mary Beth Brock glanced away from her only customer, a thin woman in an oversize coat who stood with her shoulders hunched as if she were cold.

When Mary Beth caught sight of Annie, she mimed shocked surprise. Annie offered her a grin in return. It wasn't often that she beat everyone to the shop on the day of a Hook and Needle Club meeting. In fact, Annie was often the last to arrive. It wasn't that the Hook and Needle Club meetings weren't important to her. They were. But she often found herself delayed through circumstances beyond her control. Today, though, it was smooth sailing with no last-minute phone calls or minor catastrophes.

She drifted over to the crochet pattern books and began leafing through them. One reason she'd been especially careful to arrive early was to look for a very specific kind of crochet pattern. Her twin grandchildren wanted the same Easter present: animal caps with flaps that hung down over their ears. Apparently, they were all the rage at their elementary school. Her daughter, LeeAnn, had called over the weekend just so Joanna could tell her that she wanted a puppy cap and John wanted one in the form of a monkey.

After flipping through all the books and coming up

empty-handed, Annie wandered over to the counter. The thin woman was still leaning over, looking at a yarn catalog as Mary Beth flipped through it. Finally they closed the catalog and Mary Beth said, "That's the last one I have. Why don't you give me your email address, and I'll send you a note if we get a catalog with yarn that color?"

"That would be helpful," the woman said as she wrote on the back of one of Mary Beth's business cards.

"Annie," Mary Beth said with a bright smile, "I'd like you to meet Ivy Beckett. Ivy knew your grandmother. This is Annie Dawson."

The thin woman smiled up at Annie. She was as short as Mary Beth, though Mary Beth was definitely stouter. "I would have recognized you anywhere," Ivy said softly. "Betsy showed me pictures of you many times." Then the thin woman laughed, making her look much younger as her face lit up. "In fact, I saw you in nappies once or twice."

"Oh, no," Annie said, chuckling. "I hope Gram didn't pull out those particular photos for everyone!"

"No, actually, the baby photos were part of her showing me how Grey Gables had changed through the years. I remember when she set out the azaleas in the front yard. She called them her 'Annie flowers' because they grow both in the South and up here."

"So you must have lived in Stony Point for years," said Annie. "I'm surprised we haven't bumped into each other before."

Ivy's smile faded a little, and Annie noticed that her eyes looked sad. "I'm not very social, really."

The jingle of the bell drew their attention as Stella

Brickson swept in looking every inch the matriarch with her perfectly set gray hair and beautiful brocade jacket. Swept along in Stella's wake were Kate Stevens and a stranger with ash blond hair in tight curls. Ivy whispered something to Mary Beth and hurried toward the door. "It was nice to meet you, Ivy," Annie called after her.

Ivy looked back and nodded, but didn't pause. Kate held the door open for the flustered woman. "Have a good day," Kate said.

Annie heard Ivy murmur something as she ducked out of the store, but Annie couldn't make it out.

"We seem to have frightened her off," Kate said.

"That woman is afraid of her own shadow," Stella said dismissively.

"But she's very sweet," Kate said.

"That's true," Mary Beth added, "and she adored Betsy." Mary Beth turned her cheery pixie face toward Annie. "Ivy spent a lot of time at Grey Gables and even did some gardening for Betsy when she began having trouble keeping up with it. I expect she had a hand in planting those azaleas that she mentioned. Betsy never got tired of adding color to the yard. You know your grandmother loved her garden."

The stranger who had come in with Kate and Stella peered owlishly up at Annie through very round glasses. "You're Betsy Holden's granddaughter? I've been meaning to talk to you about your home."

Annie looked at the woman in surprise. "My home?"

"Yes, I'm Nancy Breaker, the president of the Stony Point Garden Club, and we're planning an early-summer parade of homes this year. We've never done one before.

Anyway, I've seen how much work you've put into bringing Grey Gables back to the beautiful condition in which Betsy kept it years ago. The house and garden had grown so run-down, but it's quite lovely now. I know it would be a popular part of the tour. Will you let us add you in? You may opt for a quiet strolling tour of the outside grounds—maybe with some light refreshments set up under your maples. That would be very nice. Or if you're open to it, we can actually take people inside to see the restoration you've done. I hear it's lovely. The money we raise will be used for a very good cause."

"Oh?" Annie still felt a little overwhelmed by Nancy's cheerful, but forceful, personality.

"Yes, we're raising money to do some major landscaping in the Town Square," she said.

"I don't know, Nancy," Mary Beth said. "I think the Town Square looks lovely now."

"Yes, yes. The grass is nice—don't get me wrong—but I believe we could do so much more," the woman said quickly. "We could make the space a bit more formal, reflecting the more cultured element of Stony Point. We'd like to add an heirloom rose garden to the grounds. Each rose will have a little plaque telling its type. And we can sell cuttings once a year to help maintain the garden."

"You're wanting to put a formal rose garden on the grounds where kids play football and Frisbee in the summer?" Mary Beth asked.

The woman looked pained. "The children have the park. I've often thought it would be best if we discouraged such horseplay on the Town Square. Not everything has to be a children's playground." She turned back to Annie and said,

"So, may we include Grey Gables? I know Betsy would have wanted her home to be on the tour. She and I were very good friends. I often bumped into her at the grocery, and we talked and talked about flowers and such."

"You were close?" Stella said doubtfully. "Tell us, Annie, did Betsy ever mention Nancy to you?"

"Um." Annie didn't know what to say. No, her grandmother hadn't mentioned Nancy to her, but she hadn't mentioned a great many of the people Annie had met since coming to Stony Point—particularly people who had entrusted Gram with their deepest secrets.

""That's not important," Nancy said. "The question is, will you honor your grandmother's beautiful home by putting it on the tour?"

"I'll need to think about it," Annie said, growing annoyed that the woman was trying to use Betsy as a bargaining point. Gram did love Grey Gables. Annie knew that was true and that she had been proud of the house. But she couldn't picture Gram wanting to put the house on the tour. She never sought out accolades for her work. "When will the tour be held?"

"Late June. We haven't picked a date. You think about it, and I'll call you. I really have to be going; I need to speak with some other people." Then she paused and reached into her oversize leather purse. She pulled out business cards. "Here is my card, in case you want to call me instead of waiting for me to call you. Here's one for everyone." She thrust a card into Annie's hand and then turned and tried to push one onto Stella. The older woman simply glared at Nancy until she gave up.

"Nancy?" Mary Beth injected, before the woman ruffled Stella's feathers any further. "Did you come in to shop for something?"

The other woman blinked at Mary Beth. "Oh, not today. Though I do need to pick up some thread for doilies. I'll need lots of doilies for my house by June. Plus, I want to have extras in case anyone on the tour wants a few. But I really have to go talk to a few other homeowners." She turned to Annie again. "I'll be calling you."

Then she turned and bustled out of the store.

Annie watched as the little woman turned and hurried down the street. "I feel just a little bit like I was run over."

Mary Beth laughed. "Nancy has that effect on people."

2

Stella looked annoyed as she glared at the now-closed door. "Thank goodness that tiresome woman spotted you, Annie," she said. "She drove me half mad demanding I include my home on her silly tour. As if I want a bunch of strangers gawking at my home!"

"I'm sure she meant the invitation to be flattering," Kate said soothingly.

Stella just harrumphed. "Well, she'd better not add me without my permission. The first time her silly tour bus stops in front of my yard, I'll have Jason call the police and then throw rocks."

Annie smiled at the thought of Stella's calm driver standing in the yard and throwing rocks at a tour bus.

"She does have a point about both your homes," Kate said. "I'm still amazed at all you've done to bring Grey Gables back to its former state, Annie."

Annie thanked her quietly, feeling again the pang of guilt over how much tender loving care Grey Gables had needed once Annie inherited the old Victorian home. She'd largely lost touch with Betsy in the last year of her grandmother's life. They still talked on the phone regularly, but it was usually about what Annie was going through since her husband Wayne's sudden death. Annie had no idea her grandmother was declining so rapidly until it was too late.

Gram had always sounded so cheerful and full of energy when Annie spoke to her on the phone, and Annie had been distracted by the terrible pain over losing Wayne.

She sighed. There was no point dwelling on things she couldn't change. Four years had passed since Wayne's heart attack had ripped him from her life, and three since Annie had received the fateful call about Betsy's passing, She had moved to Stony Point, Maine, with the intention of settling her grandmother's estate, putting Grey Gables in order and up for sale, and then moving back to her native Texas. That was before clearing out the attic at Grey Gables had led her on a series of mysterious adventures—and before she had fallen in love again with the little fishing village. With a mental shake, she turned her attention pointedly back to the conversation.

"You know, I expect it was Nancy who scared poor Ivy off," Mary Beth said. "Nancy can be like a bulldog when she wants something. I sometimes feel a bit like running and hiding when she pops in."

"I would have guessed that I'd met just about all the permanent residents of Stony Point by now," Annie said, "and then today I'm introduced to two I'd never met. I guess it's not as small as I thought."

"It's a wonder you haven't run into Nancy by now, but maybe it's more like a blessing." Mary Beth said. "Ivy is definitely easier to overlook."

"Ivy's looking very thin," Kate said, turning to Mary Beth. "You don't suppose she's been sick? She's so alone, I can't imagine who she'd turn to if she had health issues."

"Some people just don't know how to ask for help," Stella said. "Ivy may be one of those."

Annie looked skeptically at Stella. She'd grown very fond of the slightly aloof older woman, but Stella definitely wasn't one to throw out the welcome mat in Stony Point. Still, Annie was amazed someone could stay on the fringes of Stony Point society for years—overall, this was a town that made a person feel very much at home and very much a part of everything.

"You know, at one time Betsy had Ivy nearly convinced to join us for a Hook and Needle Club meeting," Mary Beth said. "Betsy was so excited about it."

"But Ivy didn't come to the meeting, did she?" Stella asked. "Betsy was always a little too optimistic."

"I think Ivy had a good reason." Mary Beth's brow wrinkled as she tried to remember. "I don't remember what it was ... maybe she was sick?"

"I can't remember either," Kate said.

"Does she do much needlework?" Annie asked.

"I'm not really sure," Mary Beth said. "She has a lovely sense of color, but she buys the oddest supplies sometimes. I've really never figured out what type of needlework she does. She never buys patterns, and when I've asked, she tends to skirt the question."

Stella sniffed. "The girl won't even share what *craft* she does. How could we ever feel completely comfortable with someone that secretive?"

Annie turned and looked at Stella in surprise, remembering the big secret Stella had hidden from the group for years until Annie came along.

"Ivy is always very generous whenever there's any kind of need," Mary Beth said loyally, giving Stella a bit of a glare. "She's just shy."

Stella sniffed. "Kate is shy, and you don't see her dashing around like a rabbit with a hawk after her." Stella's tone softened a little. "I must admit, if I had to choose between spending time with Ivy or Nancy, I would choose Ivy every time. At least she's not pushy!"

Before anyone else could speak, the door jingled again and Gwendolyn Palmer came in. As always, Gwen was dressed in a perfectly coordinated outfit that set off her slender frame well. "Who's not pushy?" she asked.

"It's not so much who isn't, but who is," Stella said, sniffing. "Has the Garden Club harassed you about putting Wedgwood on their ridiculous tour of homes yet?"

"No," Gwen said. "Though I expect John would love the idea. He's happiest when we're right in the middle of all the social whirl."

The group continued to chat about the tour of homes as they drifted over to the ring of comfortable chairs where the Hook and Needle Club always met. Annie settled into a chair, still trying to decide if she liked the idea of having Grey Gables on some kind of tour. It sounded like a lot of work.

"Since the shop is empty, I can come and sit with everyone for a while," Mary Beth said as she slipped into the chair beside Annie.

Peggy Carson and Alice MacFarlane came in, laughing together. As she sat, Peggy turned toward Stella and grinned. "Did you really wade through a swamp in South Carolina to save Alice last fall?"

"I most certainly did not," Stella said. "I am hardly likely to ruin perfectly good clothes in a swamp! The ground on that island was only slightly soft." Then she turned her sharp glance toward Alice. "I *thought* we decided not to talk about that trip again!"

Alice's face was a perfect portrait of mock innocence as she settled into her seat in the circle. "I don't remember deciding that. Besides, the topic of … um … uneven ground came up. And I'm so grateful to my friends for coming to save me."

"If you would pick a less adventurous man to gad about with, you wouldn't need rescuing," Stella said.

"I don't know about that," Mary Beth responded. "As I remember, Alice and Annie got into plenty of trouble before Jim Parker came along."

"But the trouble is more fun now," Alice said, "and if you'll remember, my first kidnapping had nothing to do with Jim."

At that Kate laughed. "I believe just being able to number your kidnappings proves you live an unusually exciting life."

Annie smiled, but she shook her head ruefully as she thought about counting the times her house or car had been broken into. Her life was certainly more unpredictable now that she lived in Stony Point. The small town seemed so quiet on the outside, but Annie had come to realize that every town had its secrets. And sometimes secrets make people act irrationally.

"So," Mary Beth said, "shall we talk about projects? Is everyone busy with personal work, or do we need a group project? Don't forget it's almost time for the Spring Bazaar at the Stony Point Community Church. I'm afraid I really dropped the ball on this one. In the past, the Hook and Needle Club always had its own table, but I realize that might not be possible this year. Still, the bazaar is for a good cause. If there is any way we could possibly come up with enough things to fill a table, I'd still like to try."

"I have a small bunny purse that I made for Joanna before the twins called to tell me they want caps for Easter," Annie said. "I could put that in the bazaar."

"Caps?" Mary Beth said.

"They want animal caps with side flaps and strings that can tie under your chin. Joanna wants a puppy cap, and John wants one that looks like a monkey. I didn't find a pattern for that yet, though."

"Won't a cap with earflaps be a little hot in Texas, especially in the spring?" Alice asked.

"We have cool spring days down there," Annie insisted. "Of course, we don't have a lot of them, and I don't remember ever having icy ears until I moved here." Then she grinned. "Actually, they'll probably end up with sweaty heads, but that's what they asked for."

"I think I have a book that could work for the caps," Mary Beth said. "I'll show you after the meeting. A child's purse would be good for the bazaar. Anyone else? It might be a good idea to bring the things for the bazaar here. That way, if we don't end up with enough for a whole table, I can still carry them over to the church and leave them with the committee to go on one of their general donation tables."

"It's easiest for me to bring things here," Peggy said. "Time is so tight, especially with Emily in dance classes now. I seem to be rushing from one place to another all the time. But I am almost finished with a darling cathedral squares pillow top that should be great for the bazaar. I was making it for my aunt, but I just found out that she has redecorated and the colors don't go at all. I also have some crazy-quilt pincushions I made with some of my scraps. I made one for me, and they were so cute that I ended up making a bunch for Christmas." She grinned sheepishly. "I guess I overdid it a little."

"I can whip up some doll clothes," Gwen said. "They always sell well at bazaars."

"I could do that too," Kate added. "I actually have some patterns somewhere from when Vanessa was going through the doll stage."

"It sounds like we can fill a small table pretty well," Alice said. "I know I could do a few bookmarks. They shouldn't take long to cross-stitch."

"I could do some of those fuzzy scarves that I've seen on the teens in town," Stella said. "It's a fairly quick knit, and I saw you have some lovely colors in that textured yarn."

Mary Beth asked for everyone to bring their donations to the shop by the next Hook and Needle Club meeting if at all possible. That way she could plan the size of table they would need at the bazaar. Then, any stragglers could be dropped off at the shop after that.

"I can carry the things over to the church when I go to bell practice," Mary Beth said. "I know the storage room where the committee is keeping everything."

"Vanessa and I will lend a hand," Kate said, "so Mary Beth doesn't end up feeling like a pack mule."

"Bell practice?" Peggy said. "I always thought the church bell rang itself."

Mary Beth laughed. "It does, thank goodness. Can you picture me hanging from a bell rope like Quasimodo? No, we play handbells. A group of us who aren't exactly gifted singers are trying to form a bell choir. It sounded like a great idea when someone suggested it, but playing handbells is much harder than it looks."

"We had a bell choir in Brookfield," Annie said. "I always enjoyed hearing them during the holiday programs."

"We aren't really at the point where anyone would enjoying hearing us," Mary Beth said. "Which is why we need the practice. But it does mean I'm at the church two extra times a week, so it's easy for me to take a box of bazaar items."

"Is your bell choir going to perform for Easter service?" Alice asked. "I think I'd enjoy hearing that."

"That was the original goal, but you haven't heard us play." Mary Beth rolled her eyes and shook her head. "I think it's probably more realistic to plan on hearing us for the Christmas service."

"That would certainly give you plenty of time to practice," Alice said with a laugh.

"And yet, still not too much," Mary Beth said.

Annie smiled at her friends' banter, and then she suddenly had a surprising thought. Up until now, it seemed that nearly every community project in Stony Point had required a trip to the attic at Grey Gables for something. And every trip to the attic seemed to turn up a mystery. But finally, here was something that should keep her out of the attic and mystery free for a while. Annie smiled. As much as she enjoyed puzzling over the many Stony Point mysteries, she was ready for a nice quiet spring.

~ 3 ~

After the Hook and Needle Club meeting, Peggy rushed off to get to work at The Cup & Saucer before her boss, Jeff, launched a search party. Mary Beth stood and turned to Annie, "I am almost sure I've seen a book that has the animal caps you need. I culled my pattern books last week of everything that looked a little shopworn, and they're all in the back room waiting for me to tag them for a clearance sale. I think that's where I saw the book. So let me go check—if you don't mind waiting."

"I don't mind," Annie assured her. She watched as Mary Beth hurried to the back room, walking with quick strides. Even though Mary Beth was more than ten years older than her, Annie often wished she had her energy. Annie settled back in her seat to wait. She'd seen Mary Beth's back room more than once or twice, and knew nothing was likely to be found back there very quickly.

She turned to look at Alice, who was carefully folding a large piece of cross-stitch canvas. "That looks like a big project," Annie said.

"It's a new cover for my party book," Alice answered. "The old one is nearly in tatters." Alice sold Divine Décor products and Princessa jewelry in home parties all over Stony Point and its environs. Annie mentally counted Alice as another high-energy businessperson. Between Mary

Beth and Alice, Annie sometimes felt a bit like a slug, even though she tended to keep busy herself, between her work on Grey Gables and the almost endless projects that the Hook and Needle Club took part in—not to mention the mysteries that kept popping up when Annie least expected them.

"I'd love to catch up on what you've been doing lately," Annie said. "Would you like to have lunch? We could go to the diner."

"That would be great," Alice agreed, "if you don't mind a short detour. I need to stop by the library, but it really shouldn't take long."

"Doing some research for Jim?" Annie asked with interest. Jim Parker, the handsome photographer who came to Stony Point often to spend time with Alice, tended to attract nearly as many mysteries as Annie's attic. Annie would be happy to take a minor role in someone else's mystery for a change.

Alice shook her head. "No, he's off working on a draft of his next book. He does this mad writer thing where he turns hermit and just bangs on the computer keyboard and mutters darkly. I don't mind missing out on that."

"Doesn't sound like a spectator sport," Annie said.

"And that's why there are no reality shows where they film writers at work," Alice said. "At any rate, I just need to drop off a Divine Décor catalog. Josephine Booth wants one, and she only volunteers half days on Tuesdays."

"How are you doing with your parties?" Annie asked. She was constantly surprised that Alice managed to make enough on her Divine Décor and Princessa jewelry sales to survive. Annie couldn't imagine trying to sell things regularly. Although Annie's dear husband Wayne had been an amazing car salesman, Annie hadn't even been able to sell Girl Scout cookies. She always lost interest in the product, getting caught up instead listening to the dreams and problems people shared when she talked to them. Wayne often teased her that she was the ultimate people person; she never met a person who didn't interest her.

"Actually, it's going great right now," Alice answered. "This is normally a slow time—a lull between the Christmas gift-buying rush and the surge that I always see when the tourists arrive—but I've been saved this spring by a number of people doing small redecorating projects."

"I'd go crazy trying to budget around inconsistent income like that," Annie said.

"It's a challenge," Alice admitted, "but I'm used to it."

Mary Beth hurried out of the backroom with a cap pattern book in hand. "I found it! This was my last one of these from the holidays last year," she said. "I remembered that I put it in the back because the cover is a little torn. I can give you a discount for that."

"I'll just be happy if it has the animals," Annie said. She took the book and leafed through. It had a darling puppy, a kitten, a panda bear, and a teddy bear. "Oh no. It doesn't have a monkey. John was really specific about that."

Kate peeked over Annie's shoulder. "You could alter the panda bear to be a monkey. Just move the ears down to the side and use the big puppy eyes. And I would switch colors for the whole face; just use the eye patch and muzzle color directions together."

"Oh my," Annie said. "That sounds complicated. I normally just follow the directions, very slowly and carefully."

Kate was an amazing designer, but one of the side effects of underestimating her own talent was that she tended to expect everyone to be able to do what she did. She gave Annie an encouraging smile. "It sounds harder than it would be. Why don't you do the puppy first, and then I can walk you through the changes for the monkey."

"OK—that sounds good," Annie said. With Kate's help, she bought the yarn for both hats and then headed out of the shop with Alice.

Alice glanced over at Annie. "You know, you're much better at crochet than you think you are. You really need to give yourself more credit."

"I don't know," Annie said. "I'm OK on simple patterns and baby blankets, but anything I've done that was complicated involved a lot of hand-holding from Kate."

"Kate is incredible," Alice agreed. "I'm glad her design work is starting to get some recognition. I'd take up crochet if I thought I could add the kind of gorgeous things to my wardrobe that she makes for herself and Vanessa."

Annie agreed. As they walked down the sidewalk, Annie looked out over the Town Square. The winter-bare trees were beginning to show glimpses of green near the tips of the branches, and every lawn seemed dotted with crocus blooms. The air was unseasonably warm, which was quite a surprise since winter was usually in no hurry to leave Maine. "Do you think we'll have a mild spring?" she asked.

Alice laughed. "This is Maine. There is no telling what kind of weather we'll have—other than unpredictable. I've always said New England meteorologists make weather predictions by throwing darts at a list of possible forecasts."

When they reached the beautiful old Greek Revival–
style building that housed the Stony Point Public Library,
Annie reached out and patted one of the tall columns.

"What was that for?" Alice asked.

Annie shrugged. "I don't know. The library just always
feels like an old friend when we visit. I remember coming
here as a kid with Gram and carrying out all the books I
could carry." Then she smiled sheepishly. "Wayne always
teased me about treating inanimate objects like pets, especially my car."

"Hey, I wash my car, feed it gas and oil," Alice said, "and
I worry anytime it coughs or hiccups. How is that different
from having a pet?"

"Well, your convertible probably doesn't sit on your
chest to wake you up in the morning," Annie said.

"Ah, the famous kitty alarm clock. Boots has favored
me with that one a few times when I've looked after her,"
Alice said, and then she gestured at the tall columns of the
library. "I'm not surprised you're emotionally attached to
the library. You always were crazy for books. I should have
spent more time reading as a kid, but I was a little too busy
turning my mom's hair gray."

Annie laughed. "I suspect our adventures caused more
than a few gray streaks for Gram too. Until you and I met,
Gram was always telling me I should get my nose out of
books long enough to go outside and live a little. She quit
saying that about the third time we were ushered home by
an irate adult."

"Adults had no sense of humor back then," Alice said.
"What's life without some real adventure? Though our

adventures these days get a little too exciting. I've come to love curling up with a good safe book now and then—especially a mystery!"

They walked through the multipaned glass doors at the entrance. Just as the hush of the library surrounded them, Annie's stomach grumbled loudly. Both women burst into giggles. "I guess we'd better hurry in here," Alice said.

"No, really, I can wait," Annie said, pressing a hand against her middle. "I'm not ruled by my stomach." Then she winced when her stomach growled again as if to argue the point.

Still smiling, the two women walked to the front desk where all the library workers seemed to be gathered in a cluster. "What's up?" Alice asked as they approached.

"Someone left us a present," Josephine Booth said. "I found it in the children's section." She gestured at the circulation desk.

An old book lay open on the desk. Annie could see it was a shabby copy of *Alice in Wonderland*. The book lay open to a page with an illustration of a grinning Cheshire cat peering down at the little girl, Alice. On the page opposite the illustration, someone had cut a cubby out of the center of the rest of the pages. From that cutout, a grinning needle-felted orange cat in a wild top hat seemed frozen in the act of climbing out.

Annie leaned closer to see the perfect details of the cat's wide toothy smile and the tiny-size card tucked into the hatband. She saw that one of the cat's paws held the handle of a tiny teacup. "The detail is amazing," she said.

"Who made it?" Alice asked.

"We don't know," said Grace Emory, one of the reference librarians. "It had this card but no signature." She held up a small stiff square of cream-color paper. In careful hand lettering, it read, "A book is a kind of mad and wonderful dream. Thank you for years of dreaming."

"Wow," Annie said. "It must be from someone who loves the library."

"Well, we certainly love this." Valerie Duffy, the other reference librarian, touched the tiny cat gently on the nose with one finger.

"You know," Josephine said. "I recognize this book."

"It's *Alice in Wonderland*," Grace said drily. "We all recognize it."

Josephine gave Grace a reproving glance. "No, I mean I recognize *this* copy. It was in the Friends of the Library book sale last fall. I remember checking to see if it was valuable, since it's so old."

"Was it?" Alice asked.

"No," Josephine said, shaking her head. "It wasn't all that old, just badly abused. I believe there were even some pages missing. I'm surprised it sold."

"Do you know who bought it?" Annie asked.

Josephine shook her head. "I didn't handle sales. Even if I had, there were so many people and so many books, I might not have noticed."

Annie remembered how packed that sale had been. She'd gotten a great bargain on books for herself and a few really nice children's books for the twins.

"Well, it certainly is a lovely gift," Valerie said, "but we'll have to put it in one of the display cases. I don't think it would last long on an open shelf in the children's section."

"That was a scary place to leave it," Josephine agreed. "If I hadn't found it before school let out, it might have been more than a little damaged by the time we saw it."

"Maybe the giver has a specific reason for leaving it in the children's section," Annie suggested.

"I suppose she could be a mom," Josephine said, "even though I'm impressed that any mom would have the time to do this kind of amazing work."

"Maybe it's a teacher," Valerie said. "They use the children's section a lot."

"This is all very mysterious," Grace said.

Alice turned to Annie with a grin. "Wow, a mystery," she said. "And we didn't even have to go to your attic to find it!"

— 4 —

nnie spent the next several days working on the puppy cap for Joanna. She wanted to have it finished in time for the next Hook and Needle Club meeting, so she'd feel ready to understand the changes needed for the monkey one. All the crocheting kept her indoors most days, though she cast longing glances at the spring sunshine through the windows more than once.

She'd had to respond to two calls from that persistent woman with the Garden Club, and once when she looked out the window, she saw a car stop in front of the house so someone could lean out the passenger window and take photos of Grey Gables. Annie wasn't sure it was related to the Garden Club, but she suspected as much.

She wondered if it wouldn't just be easier to agree to let them put her house on the tour. Still, she simply couldn't decide. She loved working in her yard and making it as beautiful as she could, but did she really want strangers intruding on her privacy? More and more, she felt like she didn't. Plus, her natural stubbornness hated to give in to such aggressive pushiness.

On the morning that she spotted the stranger taking photos of her house, Annie had returned to her crocheting with her nerves humming with annoyance. Her stitch tension had tightened as a result, forcing her to pull out stitches and practice a few deep breaths to calm herself.

Between her nerves and the difficulty of doing so many color changes, the little cap went much slower than she'd hoped. She suspected Kate could probably have whipped up the cap in little more than an afternoon, but the color changes had confused her in a couple spots, and she'd had to undo rows more than once. Finally, she was able to finish the main part of the cap. The ears and flaps looked like they would be much quicker to do.

Even as she worked on the puppy cap, Annie felt the pressing deadline for the church bazaar. As cute as the bunny purse was, she felt like she ought to do more. So after a particularly frustrating episode of unraveling messed-up stitches, she took a break and dug out some of her pattern books for scrap projects. Then she gathered all the scraps of yarn left over from sweaters and afghans. She found a pattern for adorable small stuffed toys, each with a small jingle bell in the middle.

She set aside Joanna's cap for an hour and made two colorful little belled toys. By the time she finished the two simple toys, she had relaxed and tackled the puppy cap with fresh self-confidence.

Boots seemed to take the hours Annie spent on her crocheting as a challenge. The cat particularly wanted the toys with the bells. If Annie stepped away from her project bag for a minute, Boots immediately dove into it.

"Boots, cut it out!" Annie scolded when she walked back into the living room with a cup of tea and saw that her project bag had grown a fluffy gray tail—*again*. The cat stuck her head out of the bag and looked at Annie. "You better not wreck Joanna's cap."

Boots gave an innocent meow and then ducked back into the bag.

Annie set her teacup down on the small table beside the sofa. She reached into her bag and began untangling Boots from the yarn. By the time she finished, she saw that Boots had unraveled most of the last side flap for the little hat. "You're such a bad kitty," Annie scolded as she put Boots on the floor.

Boots immediately sprang back up on the couch as Annie sat down. The fluffy gray cat squeezed into Annie's lap. "You know," Annie said. "I should probably be much firmer with you."

Boots only purred loudly in reply. Annie knew better than to think she'd ever teach the spoiled cat any manners, so she just sighed and patiently reworked the earflap on Joanna's cap. She then quickly crocheted the chin strings that hung from the flaps. All she had left to do was to stitch the hat pieces together.

Annie glanced up toward the tall windows. It was a beautiful day outside. The unseasonable warm snap had hung on, and she felt the pull of the outdoors. She loved the idea of taking a walk without bundling up in her arctic gear. "It almost seems criminal to stay inside all day," she said.

Boots opened one eye before settling back to sleep.

"I know you're not going to like this," Annie said, "but I definitely want to go out." She shifted Boots from her lap as gently as she could, but still got a grumpy meow from the cat.

Annie packed up her crochet and brushed the cat hair

from her clothes. She hung her project bag on one of the pegs near the front door where she hung coats. "That should keep Joanna's cap out of prying paws."

Annie opened the front door and looked out, trying to judge the temperature. She was already wearing a sweater she'd crocheted a year ago. The thick, fuzzy yarn, in shades of blue, reminded her of the ocean. The super-soft sweater felt like she was getting a cozy hug all the time. Annie decided she would be warm enough in the spring sunshine, so she pulled the door closed and headed down the porch steps.

On a whim, Annie headed across the street where a chain was strung between two low piled-stone pillars. A gravel road led steeply up the hill. Near the gravel road, a small winding path led gently downhill toward the beach. Annie took the winding path, enjoying the sight of crocuses and snowdrops nestled in the bright green tips of the wild grasses that would line the path later in the year.

A walk on the beach in the spring, even on such a gorgeous day, was risky. The icy breeze off the water usually made beach walking a frigid experience until mid-June, but with the warm sun on her face, she decided to take the risk. She'd scout around for sea glass and watch the gulls squabble over the tiny crabs on the shore.

As soon as she reached the hard-packed sand of the rocky beach, she realized her mistake. The wind from the water was much chillier than she had expected. Annie glanced back the way she'd come, but she really wasn't ready to give up on her walk. Instead, she crossed her arms and began striding down the beach at a brisk pace, hoping it would help her stay warm.

The brisk exercise did help, but each fresh breeze threatened to chill her all over again. Annie glanced out over the waves. She loved the constant movement as each wave rose up and rushed for the shore before breaking under its own weight and collapsing into foam. It was a love she had learned early in life, on summer visits to Stony Point to stay with her grandparents at Grey Gables while her parents were on overseas missionary trips. There was a timelessness about the ebb and flow of the sea that gave Annie perspective about life. She knew she was watching the same pattern of rising water and breaking waves that the Native Americans must have seen when standing on the same beach hundreds of years before.

Offshore, she spotted something dark bobbing in the waves. She paused, squinting to try to make out details. At first, she thought it might be a rock, appearing and disappearing as the waves broke against it. But then she saw it was moving closer to shore.

Anne walked to the edge of the water, risking her shoes in the lap of the waves. Was she seeing someone's head bobbing in the surf? It might be an unseasonable warm snap, but it was still March in Maine! Surely no one would go swimming. Annie felt a sick anxiety wash over her as a thought struck her. Not everyone who walked out into the surf was going swimming. Was it someone trying to drown himself?

"Hello!" she shouted. "Hello. Is someone out there?"

She watched to see if the bobbing head might be joined by an upraised arm in response to her calls, but nothing changed except the dark object still seemed to be moving slowly closer to shore.

Annie paced the shoreline for a moment, unsure of what to do. She'd be so embarrassed if she called 911, only to find out the bobbing object was an escaped lobster-pod float or something equally innocuous.

Finally, the bobbing head came close enough for Annie to work out a bit more detail. She saw the sun glisten against slick dark skin. Two black eyes turned toward her and dripping whiskers just barely cleared the water. She'd been panicking over a seal! Annie chuckled and shook her head. This was definitely the sort of situation where she was glad to be alone on the beach so no one could see her fretting about a seal's suicide attempt.

～5～

Suddenly a shiver shook Annie. She'd stood worrying over the seal long enough for the cold to catch up with her again. She definitely needed to head home for a cup of hot chocolate and a warm cat. She turned back and strode quickly along.

In the distance, she spotted a tall figure walking toward her. Annie smiled. From the long-legged gait, she was certain she must be seeing Stony Point's mayor, Ian Butler. If Ian was out for a walk, Annie might brave the cold a little longer to walk with him. She had been so busy for the last few days that she hadn't dropped by the courthouse or run into the handsome New Englander at the diner to share a cup of coffee.

The closer Annie came to the long-legged figure, the more she realized she'd made another mistake. Though tall and slender like Ian, this man's hair was darker than Ian's salt-and-pepper hair. And the stranger tended to hunch in on himself a bit as he walked, while Ian always walked with ramrod confidence. Like Ian, the stranger had high cheekbones, though the lines in his face were harsher, and his nose was sharp as a hawk's beak.

Annie realized she'd been staring when the tall stranger looked right at her and smiled. It turned the creases in his face into laugh lines. Annie smiled back slightly.

"Excuse me for bothering you," the stranger said in a clear, refined British accent. "Could you help me?"

"I can try," Annie said. "Do you need directions?"

"Something like that," he answered, nodding his head. "I'm looking for someone. A young woman—well, I guess not terribly young anymore. About your age, I would guess. Not that you aren't young …."

Annie laughed before the man could grow any more flustered. "Do you know the woman's name?" she asked.

The man sighed, smiling a bit sheepishly. "It's Candace Caine. She writes and illustrates picture books for children. I think she may live around here. Or perhaps she visited here for a length of time."

"Her name sounds familiar. I think my grandchildren have some of her books," Annie said. "There's one about a little boy who wakes up to find a whole circus in his house, right?"

The man nodded. "Yes, that's one of her books. You see, I am her publisher in London. My name is Adam Smithfield. I've been looking for her."

"She disappeared?" Annie asked.

"Something like that," he said, his eyes sad. Annie felt a pang for the stranger. "She's gone, and I haven't been able to find her. One lead I had brought me to Stony Point, and I just arrived."

"Have you called the authorities?" Annie asked. "Our Chief Edwards is very good if you need to file a report or something."

"I'm certain no one *took* Candace," Adam said with a sigh. "Wherever she is, she is there voluntarily."

THE CATS & THE RIDDLE 35

"Oh," Annie said. "And you're looking for her for business reasons?"

Adam shook his head. "No, my reasons are completely personal. Stony Point seems to be a fairly small town. Would it be difficult for someone to move here and go unnoticed? I've always assumed it's much harder to stay anonymous in a small town. People are so much more interested in their neighbors."

Annie wasn't certain whether she should do anything to encourage the stranger's search for a woman who might not want him to find her. Her thoughts immediately went to another woman, who had come to Stony Point to blend in, disappear, and hide from a man who terrified her. Annie had nearly gotten an old friend killed when she'd gotten involved with *that* mystery. Some people had good reasons for coming to a place and vanishing, sometimes very good reasons indeed. It would be wiser, she knew, if she stayed far away from this mystery.

"No one has mentioned her moving here," she said carefully. "I would definitely have remembered."

At that the stranger looked so disappointed that Annie couldn't leave him without some sort of hope. Though she wasn't completely confident in her own ability to judge character, she did have an overwhelming desire to help whenever she saw someone hurting. "I haven't actually been living in Stony Point long enough to know everyone," she said hesitantly, hoping she wasn't making a bad decision. "You might ask at The Cup & Saucer. If she lives anywhere in Stony Point, someone there will know her. You can be sure of it." At least by sending the man toward Peggy Carson at the diner, Annie would soon have everyone in Stony Point aware of what he wanted.

"The Cup & Saucer," he echoed, his eyes bright again. "Is that a dishware store?"

Annie laughed. "No, it's a diner. It's at the corner of Main Street and Oak Lane, across from the Town Square and the library. Everyone in Stony Point goes there at least once in a while."

Suddenly the tall man seemed to notice Annie's shivering. "Oh, you're cold. Here, take my coat." He slipped out of his wool coat and wrapped it quickly around Annie before she could protest. As the warmth of the coat sank in, she thanked him. It wrapped around Annie like a kimono, and she used the belt to hold it closed against the cold. She stuffed her hands in the pockets to warm them.

Adam had turned to walk along beside Annie. "Is there a nice place to stay around here?" he asked.

"Maplehurst Inn is lovely," Annie said.

"Is it easy to find?" he asked. "I'm still having some culture shock about driving on the wrong side of the roads. The sat nav in my rental car is a great help, but sometimes I have trouble understanding her accent."

"Sat nav?"

"Um, GPS," Adam explained. "Sorry, I actually come to the United States quite often. You'd think I could get the words straight."

Annie laughed. "I've lived in the United States all my life, and some of the words I've encountered since moving from Texas to Maine have completely baffled me. But I don't think you'll have any trouble finding the inn. Once you reach Main Street, you'll soon see most of what Stony Point has to offer—including Maplehurst Inn."

They walked together in peaceful silence for a few moments. His eyes turned toward the surf several times before they reached the parking lot.

"Candace always loved the ocean," Adam said as they crossed the near empty lot. "I knew there wasn't much chance I would just bump into her on the beach today, but I guess I still hoped. And it was a lucky walk. I met you."

"Well, I hope I've helped you," Annie said. She shrugged out of the coat and handed it to him.

"I think you have," Adam said. "I feel hopeful." He opened his door and tossed the coat onto the passenger seat. Then he turned to Annie. "I don't know your name."

"Annie Dawson," she said.

"Thank you for your help, Annie Dawson."

Then Adam climbed into his car and drove away. Annie watched the car until it disappeared. Then, as she turned to head home, she spotted a worn envelope on the ground. She bent to retrieve it before the wind blew it away.

She turned the envelope over in her hands and saw it was addressed to Adam Smithfield with a London address. She brought the envelope close to her face to read the postmark. It had been mailed in Stony Point, though the return address on the envelope was from somewhere in New York City. She surmised that the envelope was what had brought Adam to Stony Point. It would be important to him. She assumed it had fallen from his coat when she'd taken it off to return it. *I'll just run it by the inn by the end of the day*, she thought.

She hurriedly climbed the long, uphill path toward Grey

Gables. The further she got from the water, the less chilly the air felt. Plus the climb helped warm her up. By the time she'd reached her house, she was slightly winded and toasty warm.

Annie walked through the front door, and Boots rushed over to thread through her legs, meowing complaints the whole time. "It's not dinnertime," Annie said firmly.

As she walked slowly, careful not to fall over the persistent cat, the phone began to ring. "Boots," she scolded, "stop it, before you trip me."

Finally she reached the low table and answered the phone with a sharp, "Hello!"

"Hi Annie," Ian's deep voice rumbled with amusement. "You sound annoyed. I hope I haven't called at a bad time."

"Sorry, Ian," Annie said as she dropped the tattered envelope onto the phone table and sank into a chair beside it. "Boots seems to be determined to trip me. I think she may be trying to kill me in hopes of inheriting everything."

Ian chuckled. "You shouldn't say that where she can hear it. You'll give her ideas."

Boots hopped up on the phone table and began knocking things off onto the floor as she paced over and around the phone. "Hold on," Annie said. "Boots is in a mood, and I need to corral her before she manages to hang up the phone on us."

She scooped up the cat and headed through the kitchen and the back of the house to the mudroom. She deposited Boots on the floor and shut her into the room. The cat's disgruntled yowls followed Annie through the kitchen as she hurried back, but had faded by the time she reached the living room. At least she wouldn't have to try to talk over the cat's complaints. She grabbed the phone and sank back into the chair again. "OK, I'm free to talk now."

"I expect Boots is not happy about whatever you just did," Ian said. "She may be plotting some kind of revenge as we speak."

"Oh, I'm sure you're right," Annie said as she curled up in the chair next to the table. "She'll let me know all about how I've wronged her, or she'll give me the feline version of the silent treatment. It never lasts though. Dinnertime fixes everything. So, what's going on?"

"I called to ask for a favor," Ian said. "I need someone to look after Tartan. I'm going out of town, and the kennel where he normally stays is full. They're doing some renovating, so only have part of the building running."

"I would be glad to have him stay here. I love Tartan," Annie said. "But if I put him and Boots in the same house, I'm not sure either of them will make it out alive."

Ian laughed again. "I don't know, I might bet on Boots. Tartan has the weight advantage, but Boots has more practice with maiming intruders to Grey Gables. Luckily, I was planning to leave Tartan here at home. I know it's a lot to ask, but I was hoping you could come over in the mornings and put Tartan outside in his run. Then you could come in the evening and put him inside in the back mudroom. His kennel is in that room, but I don't want to close him into the kennel itself—I'll just Tartan-proof the room, and it will give him a little more room to stretch out."

"Well that sounds easy enough," Annie said. "Though I didn't know you had an outside run for Tartan. I've never seen it, and I know I've seen your whole yard."

"I had Wally build it for me the second the ground thawed this year," Ian said. Wally Carson was Peggy's husband and the town's go-to guy for all handyman projects. Not only did he do excellent work, but everyone liked helping out the small family. "I'm going to do some planting this spring without Tartan unplanting behind me while I work," Ian insisted.

Annie laughed. "You could leave him inside on gardening days."

"I know, but he loves it outside, and I am a total pushover," Ian said. "He actually seems to like the run, though he hasn't been in it much. I enjoy walking him as much as I can."

"I could take him for a walk each day," Annie said. "It will be good for both of us. I could certainly use the exercise."

"Well, walking a schnauzer can be like walking a pogo stick," Ian said. "You're welcome to give it a try, but it's perfectly OK if you don't want to be quite that active!"

As Ian began listing where he kept Tartan's food and leash and various other things, Annie gently interrupted. "Why don't I just come over, and you can show me where everything is?" she asked. "I'd probably remember better with a walk-through. And I can ask questions if they come to mind."

"That would be easiest," Ian said, "if you don't mind."

Annie assured him that she was happy to help. As they ended the call, she picked up the small notepad and pen that Boots had knocked on the floor earlier. That reminded her that her cat was still shut up in the mudroom, growing more hostile by the minute. In her rush to the mudroom door and then out to the car, Annie never even noticed the faded envelope wedged between the table leg and the wall.

~6~

nnie drove up the long driveway to Ian's house, enjoying the soft green of the newly budded leaves on the trees and the occasional burst of color from a flowering tree. The breeze shook the thinner branches and made petals rain down along the road like pink and white snow.

Though Ian's house was over one hundred years old, it had aged beautifully. Ian's natural attention to detail showed in his house and yard. Annie was proud of the work she'd put into Grey Gables since she'd moved to Stony Point, but if she used Ian's place as the standard of a well-kept house, she knew Grey Gables still had a ways to go.

She parked her beloved Malibu and patted the car on the dash and then laughed at herself, remembering her conversation about inanimate pets that she'd had with Alice. She shook her head sheepishly; her affection for her car was similar to her affection for Grey Gables. Both had been given to her by someone she loved dearly and missed badly. Grey Gables was packed with memories of her grandparents and the love they'd poured out for her during the summers she stayed with them. And her old Malibu, given to her by her dear Wayne when they ran a Chevrolet dealership in Texas, reminded her of him each time she drove it.

Annie still had to blink away a few tears at times—like now—but she was able to think of Wayne with a bittersweet joy. The first couple of years after his death had been tough. She'd felt so alone with Wayne gone and then Gram passed away as well. Annie gave herself a little mental shake and got out of the car. Being part of the tightly knit community of Stony Point was an amazing blessing, and her years in Maine had been cathartic and healing. Annie focused on that as she trotted to Ian's front door, and she smiled brightly as he greeted her.

The Stony Point mayor looked good in his worn jeans, faded T-shirt, and the flannel shirt he wore over the T-shirt like a jacket.

"You look comfortable," Annie said. She had a passing thought about how unfair it was that he looked so good in jeans and faded clothes. When she put on clothes like that, she felt like a washerwoman. When Ian put them on, he looked rugged and capable.

Ian looked down at his outfit. "I'm a little scruffy today. I thought I might give Tartan a bath so you don't have to deal with a dirty dog."

"I don't think I've ever seen Tartan looking dirty," Annie said. "I always imagined he moved too fast for the dirt to settle."

Ian smiled. "He does love to run. His day is usually spent in explosions of energy followed by naps. You should see him race through the house when he's on a rip. It's the doggy version of the Indy 500. He's in nap mode at the moment, I believe. Let me show you where I keep all his things."

Ian led her down the long hall from the foyer. Annie glanced through the French doors that led to his study. She loved the cozy look of the study with its dark overstuffed furniture and soft brown carpet. Not for the first time, she wondered if Ian had remodeled after his wife, Arianna, died, or if the study had always looked so masculine since it was Ian's domain.

The hall eventually opened into the kitchen, but Ian continued past and into the mudroom. The room was mostly empty. The floor was covered in dark tile, and one wall had built-in cubbyholes for coats and boots. The rest of the room was bare except for a large dog cage with a thick foam pad inside. "This is Tartan's kennel," he said. "Again, you don't have to shut him in it. I normally do at night. He seems to like that, but I don't want him shut up as many hours as he'll need to be while I'm gone. The room offers him more area to move around and access to food and water."

"I assume this is a sudden trip?" Annie asked.

Ian's expression clouded. "Yes, my mother-in-law is in a hospice in Upstate New York. I visit when I can. Today, I got a call from Benjamin, her nephew. He said she's nearing the end, and she's asking for me." Ian sighed. "She's asking for Arianna as well. Benjamin says that every time they tell her about Arianna, she cries like it just happened. So now they've stopped telling her and are making excuses for Arianna not being there."

"That is so sad," Annie said. She reached out and gently touched his arm. Ian had become very dear to her—much more than she cared to admit. Her eyes clouded with tears again; she looked down so Ian wouldn't notice.

Ian nodded and then cleared his throat and showed Annie where he stored Tartan's dog food. As Annie was making notes, she heard the rapid click of claws on the kitchen floor just before Tartan burst into the mudroom. He caught sight of Annie and gave a happy bark before nearly bowling her over.

"Tartan!" Ian scolded as he caught the dog's collar and pulled him gently off Annie. "Sorry about that. You're one of his favorite people."

Annie leaned over and scratched Tartan's clipped ears, enjoying the velvety soft fur that covered each ear. "And he's my very favorite dog."

Ian took a leash from one of the coat hooks and clipped it to Tartan's collar, which took a couple tries because the dog was dancing with joy. "Let's go outside, and I'll show you his new run."

Tartan dashed to the end of the leash as if he intended to haul Ian out the back door by force. Annie stepped ahead and opened the door, and the dog surged through. Once they were outside, Tartan ran to Annie, then to Ian, then to the end of the leash and then gave a little jump in the air before repeating the whole routine again and again.

"Tartan makes me tired just looking at him," Annie said, which distracted Tartan from his circuit since he seemed to feel he needed to make an extra rush to Annie's side as she spoke.

"He has that affect on me now and then," Ian said chuckling. "Now you know my secret to eating at the diner every day without gaining weight. Tartan is my personal trainer."

"Ah, then I'm especially happy to look after him," Annie said. "After a long winter of eating, I can use a personal trainer."

Ian glanced at her with a slow grin. "You look great to me."

Annie felt a blush warm her face. "You definitely scored a mayoral reelection vote there, Mr. Mayor."

They crossed the well-tended backyard to a long rectangular fenced-in area. At one end, a maple overhung the fence a bit, providing some shade over an igloo-shaped doghouse. The rest of the long run was packed dirt. Beyond the run, the lawn stretched a short way before a small patch of woods began.

"I put the run way back here so Tartan could bark at squirrels and rabbits in the woods," Ian said. "Sometimes I'm amazed he doesn't go hoarse. As I said, he hasn't spent a lot of time out here as I like having him with me, but *sometimes*—well ... let's just say changing out the storm windows was much easier than usual. And I'm looking forward to getting through leaf raking in half the time this autumn."

"Oh, do you let Tartan jump in the piles?" Annie asked.

"A few," Ian admitted. "Actually most of them. He loves it so much. But this fall, I'm only going to rake leaves twice, which is about five times less than usual."

Annie grinned. "That's certainly planning ahead. I bet you were a great Boy Scout."

Ian gave the Scout salute. "Just let me know if you need help across the street."

Annie raised her eyebrows. "So you're calling me a little old lady?"

Ian shook his head. "Nope. Just saying I like being with you."

"Nice save."

Tartan dashed over to the outside fence of the run and

put his paws up on it, peering through. "Not today, boy," Ian said. "Today you stay with me."

Tartan looked back at his master, his tongue lolling in a doggie grin. Then he dropped down and dashed over to Ian for a pat.

"I can't tell you how much I appreciate this," Ian said. "I have gotten so used to taking Tartan to the kennel where they just fuss over him endlessly. I was worried about leaving him alone with a neighbor checking in on him. I only intend to be gone a couple days."

"Oh?" Annie said. "Do you know what day you'll be back?"

"Not precisely. I really won't know how long I'm staying until I'm there," he said. "Since I have you to watch Tartan, I'm leaving tomorrow evening. I'd like to make most of the drive at night to avoid some of the stop-and-go traffic. So you don't need to come check on Tartan until Sunday morning."

"Well, don't worry a bit about Tartan," Annie said, patting his arm. "I'll be happy to look after him as long as you want. Do you want me to bring in your mail too?"

"Oh, I completely forgot." Ian smacked himself lightly in the forehead. "If you don't mind, it'll save me having to get the mail stopped."

"I'll be happy to help," Annie said. "And if you think of anything else after you're gone, just give me a call. I'll do whatever you need."

Ian put his arm around her and gave her a hug, holding her close a bit longer than usual. "I appreciate that more than you know."

─ 7 ─

When Annie finally left Ian's house with a notebook full of instructions for Tartan's care, she was reminded again of her last days with Wayne. She'd always looked forward to growing old with her husband, and she imagined Ian had felt the same about Arianna. Wayne's heart attack and his last days hooked up to machines in intensive care had been terrifying for her. At the time, she'd barely believed she could survive the loss of him.

Annie wondered if the trip to the hospice would take Ian back to the tough days of his wife's passing. She suspected it would, and her heart hurt to think of Ian's pain. She was happy to watch Tartan for him, but she wished she could do more.

As she drove, Annie remembered that she needed a trip to the grocery to pick up something for supper. She really didn't feel up to bumping into anyone she knew, especially since she suspected her eyes might be a little red from the tears she'd shed at Ian's. She drove to the tiny fish market not far from the Shirt Shack and picked up some haddock fillets for supper and some cusk to make into a chowder for the weekend.

When Annie got home, she scooped up Boots at the door and gave the cat a hug. Boots tolerated the display of affection for a few minutes and then began squirming.

When Annie put Boots down, the cat marched off to the kitchen, turning to look back at Annie and meow.

"Right," Annie said. "Food before snuggles."

After tending to Boots, Annie fixed herself a lovely supper of baked fish and rice pilaf. She loved living in an area where the words "fresh fish" meant the fish was straight off the boat. Boots managed to beg a nibble or two of the haddock, though Annie tried hard to be firm.

After supper, Annie and Boots settled down on the sofa while Annie finished Joanna's cap. She felt very proud as she held it up to admire it and check for any flaws. "One down, one to go," she told a sleepy Boots before she scooped up the cat and headed off to bed.

On Saturday, Annie made several more toys for the church bazaar before giving in to the inviting spring sunshine. She spent the next few hours working on preparing her flower beds for the annuals she intended to buy. She stood with her hands on her hips and looked up hopefully at the warm spring sun. Could she dare trust the unseasonably warm days and begin planting? She longed to see cheerful little flower faces in all her beds.

Annie finally decided to get a few flats of pansies. They were so resilient and not terribly expensive if the weather decided to turn wintry again. She hopped in her Malibu and headed into town.

After loading a few flats of pansies in a kaleidoscope of colors into the backseat, she walked up the sidewalk to A Stitch in Time. She wanted to tell Kate she had completed Joanna's cap and see when her friend could spare some time to help with the monkey cap for John.

Kate and Mary Beth waved her over to the counter as soon as she opened the door. "Come and see what we found," Mary Beth said.

Kate stepped slightly to the right to make room so Annie could see the needle-felted sculpture on the counter. A fluffy calico kitten sat on a cream-color knitted pillow trimmed with dainty crocheted lace. The kitten seemed to look wistfully at Annie with wide blue eyes. "Oh, it's darling," Annie said softly. "And so real. I've seen that very look on Boots's face so many times—halfway between disgruntled and hopeful."

"Isn't it gorgeous?" Mary Beth said. "Kate found it just a few minutes ago in one of the yarn cubbies."

"I was straightening up the yarn, getting all the colors into the right cubbies and checking to see what yarn we needed to order. The kitten was tucked way in the back of the brown cubby."

"Do you have any idea who left it?" Annie asked. "It must have been someone this morning—right?"

Mary Beth shook her head. "Not necessarily. With the kitten tucked toward the back and the cubby holding mostly autumn shades of yarn, it's not one that anyone is really buying right now."

"Even if it were someone today," Kate said, "we've been crazy busy. I guess lots of people are working on spring crafts or rushing to finish last-minute bazaar donations. It could have been nearly anyone in town."

"Did you know a needle-felted cat was found at the library?" Annie asked.

Mary Beth nodded. "I've seen it in the case in the

children's section. Grace is practically ordering every patron to look at it. It's adorable, but I like ours better."

"Because it's ours," Kate added.

"That does help," Mary Beth admitted.

"The one at the library had a note," Annie said. "Did you find a note with this kitten?"

Mary Beth and Kate both looked at one another. "I completely forgot that the library cat had a note," Mary Beth said. "You didn't find a note with this one—right, Kate?"

"I didn't see one," Kate said, "but I didn't take out all the yarn in the cubby. Once I found the little cat, I haven't done much of anything except admire it. There could be a note still hiding in the cubby, I suppose."

The three women hurried over for a brief treasure hunt and quickly unearthed a card with the same lovely hand lettering as the library note. "Handmade Is Love Made. Thank you."

"That's beautiful," Mary Beth said quietly. "A sentiment like that certainly sounds like it's one of our usual customers, don't you think?"

"Do you know of anyone who does needle felting?" Annie asked. "That is amazing work. I know I couldn't do it."

Kate looked closely at the kitten. "Stella did some simple needle-felted flowers to go on a knitted jacket once. She inspired me, and I've done some really easy stuff for my designs. Needle felting is easier than it looks, but something like this takes real talent. About the best I can manage is a cute strawberry or ladybug."

"I've tried a little bit of everything," Mary Beth said, "so that I can talk about anything with customers. But I'm with Kate. About the most ambitious needle felting I could do would be a heart. I carry a few simple supplies, but they haven't been big sellers."

"So far, there have been two cat sculptures," Annie said. "So apparently we're looking for an artist who loves cats and reading and crafts." She reached out and touched the tiny kitten's soft tail. "It's amazing to think there could be such an amazing artist hiding in Stony Point and no one knows who it is."

"Well ..." Mary Beth said, glancing in Kate's direction, "we know some artists can be too shy to share their talents if someone doesn't *make* them."

Annie laughed. "So we're back to looking for Kate?"

Kate held up her hands. "I definitely could not make anything like that. I promise that I am not the mystery artist!" Then she smiled a little sheepishly. "In fact, my first efforts at needle felting looked more like something a cat coughed up. I've gotten a little better, but like I said, I'm at the ladybug and strawberry level—I definitely couldn't make a little cat that looks like it's about to get up and prance around."

"You know what we have here," Mary Beth said. "A mystery! Someone has dropped a mystery right here at A Stitch in Time. I think we should make this mystery a Hook and Needle Club project."

"Everyone will certainly enjoy a new mystery," Kate agreed.

"Well, if we find who is making these little treasures, we'll probably have to swear everyone to secrecy," Annie said. "It looks like this artist wants to keep it a secret, or maybe a surprise. I wouldn't want to spoil that."

"That shouldn't be a problem," Mary Beth said cheerfully. "We can keep it secret."

Annie looked at her friend a little doubtfully. Between Mary Beth and Peggy, secret sharing was a much bigger gift than secret keeping. Still, she knew her friends wouldn't want to hurt anyone, so she decided not to voice her concerns any further—for now.

When Annie got home, she set out all the pansies, singing quietly to herself as she worked. She loved pansies. They added so many different colors to the garden, and each plant seemed to smile up at her. Then she cleaned up and started her chowder. The delicious smell of the soup acted like a siren call for Boots, and the cat hung around the kitchen in case something delicious should fall to the floor. Annie turned on the oven to heat up a crusty loaf of French bread she'd picked up at Magruder's Groceries earlier in the week. She loved crusty bread with chowder.

The soup was as wonderful as Annie had hoped, with the tender fish in contrast to the slightly firm potatoes, all bathed in a smooth creamy soup and complemented by the crunch of the sliced French bread. She was happy to have leftovers to freeze since she knew the soup would only get better with time.

As she was washing the dishes, the phone rang. Assuming it was Ian with last-minute Tartan instructions, Annie wiped her hands quickly on a towel as she hurried into the living room and picked up the phone. "Hello?"

"Oh, Mom!" her daughter, LeeAnn, cried, her voice thick. "We've had the most horrible day."

Annie felt a jolt of sick worry rush through her. "Are the twins OK?"

"Yes, we're all fine. It's not that kind of horrible," LeeAnn reassured her. "Herb's boss called him into his office at the end of work today. The company is downsizing, and they've let Herb go. I don't understand it. The men they're keeping have so much less experience and skill than Herb."

"But I suspect they also make less money," Annie said, finishing the thought for her.

LeeAnn sighed. "Yes, basically, I imagine that's it. I'm so worried. Herb is wonderful at what he does, but the job market is really tough right now, you know? We've lost so many companies in our area in the last couple of years."

"Do you need my help?" Annie asked. "I have some savings and a few investments that your father made, and I also have that nest egg of proceeds from the sale of the dealership. They're all doing pretty well. If you need anything to tide you over for a while, I can send a check or wire the money."

"Oh, no," LeeAnn said hurriedly. "We have savings. Herb is really careful about things like that. He is getting a nice severance package too. It certainly doesn't help that my car is in the shop, and the parts are taking forever to get. It's just ... well, I'm worried, and I don't want to rain all my worries down on Herb when he's already feeling bad enough. You know how important it is to him to be a good provider for me and the twins. He doesn't need to hear anything but support from me right now. So I guess I called the one person I could just unload on—sorry."

"That's OK, sweetheart," Annie said. "That's what moms are for."

"I appreciate that," LeeAnn said. "I need to settle down and start looking at our budget. I need to decide which things we can do without for a while. Hey, maybe it's a good thing that the car is in the shop. Think of the gas we'll save with just one car for a while."

"Don't try to take on too much all at once," Annie said. "Everything doesn't have to be settled in one day."

"I know," LeeAnn said. "You know me. I want to get everything done at once because it makes me feel less out of control."

"I do know you, and I totally understand how you feel. That kind of uncertainty is frightening," Anne said. "But you don't have to be in control *all* the time. And sometimes a situation that looks really bad is actually a chance for positive change if you can just let it happen."

Annie could practically see her daughter nodding. "Now you sound like Pastor Mitchell," said LeeAnn. "Remember all the times he's preached on letting go so God can take control?"

"That's so important and so hard to do," Annie said quietly. "But we know God has a plan."

"Right," LeeAnn said quietly. "Now if I can just keep from falling into total panic until we find out what it is."

"Well, if you need anything, you call," Annie said. "You know you have my prayers, but if you need anything tangible like money, you let me know about that too. I'd offer to loan you my car, but I don't think that would quite work out."

LeeAnn laughed. "Though picking it up in Stony Point might be fun. I know the twins would be wild about that."

"They certainly have wild tastes in Easter presents,"

Annie said. "I managed to finish Joanna's puppy cap, and I think I should be able to do John's monkey cap with only a few bouts of total panic."

"I know they'll be showing them off proudly all over school."

"I'll just be happy if the monkey doesn't end up looking like a panda puppy." Annie explained how she and Kate hoped to adapt the pattern.

"Well, if anyone can sort it out, it's Kate," LeeAnn said. "I'm still getting compliments on the jacket she made that you gave me for my birthday. Thanks again, Mom."

"You already thanked me for the jacket," Annie said. "Repeatedly."

"It's not just for the jacket," LeeAnn said. "Just talking to you always makes me feel better. I wish we lived closer."

"That would be lovely," Annie said, "but even when we did, we didn't see each other all that often."

"I tried."

"I wasn't scolding you," Annie said. "You have a family now, and you're supposed to put them first. I wouldn't have it any other way. Honestly, I'm constantly amazed by all the things you manage to accomplish. And you get up here to visit, and I get down there to see you too. I promise, I won't let the twins or you feel like I'm losing touch."

"I know. Really I do. You know, we ought to come for a visit now," LeeAnn said wryly. "At least Herb couldn't say he's too busy at work."

"Do you want me to send money for airline tickets?" Annie asked, only half joking. She loved the idea of seeing the twins as much as possible. Annie knew all too well how quickly children grow up, despite her assurances that they wouldn't grow up without her.

"I'll get back to you on that," LeeAnn said distractedly. "It was good to talk to you, Mom. You put a lot of things in perspective for me. I need to go get the twins moving along towards bed, but I'll call again soon. I think I'm going to need a lot of hand-holding."

"My hand is always free," Annie said. When LeeAnn hung up, Annie bowed her head and said a prayer for her daughter and the family. Whatever God wanted for them, she just trusted that it would be a good thing in the end.

— 8 —

The next morning, Annie got up early and rushed over to Ian's to let Tartan out into his run. "I promise I'll come back after church and walk you," she told the excited dog.

Since she couldn't leave without at least petting Tartan at length, she was a little behind schedule when she got home and had to dress quickly for church. She was just brushing stray cat hair from her delicately patterned floral dress and jacket when the phone rang. "I'm certainly popular lately," she murmured as she picked it up.

"Annie, I need your help," Alice said. "I have made too many apple cinnamon muffins, and I need someone to help me eat them. Can I bring a few over? We could have a little breakfast before church."

"You know I'm here to help my dear friend in her time of need," Annie joked. "Sounds delicious, especially since I didn't have a chance to fix anything. You'll be saving me from embarrassing stomach growling during the quiet prayerful moments at church. I'll put the coffee on."

It only took a few minutes for Alice to gather her muffins into a cloth-lined basket and make the walk between her house and Annie's. Alice lived in a miniature version of Grey Gables, as it had once been the carriage house when both houses were part of a single large property. She had rented the carriage house for years, all the way back to when Betsy was still alive, but she had just recently closed the deal to purchase it.

Annie let Alice in quickly to keep Boots from making a dash for the yard. "I think Boots is getting spring fever," Annie complained. "Though she's a little old and spayed to be looking for a boyfriend."

Alice laughed as she followed Annie to the kitchen. "I don't know if anyone is ever too old for a little romance."

"Well, cat romance maybe."

Annie poured tall mugs of coffee for them and carried them to the table. Then she sat and broke a piece from a muffin, moaning at the first bite of cinnamon and apple. "You're baking is always so good," she said.

"I get lots of practice," Alice said. "I sometimes think the muffins and coffee cakes are as important to my Devine Décor parties as the actual products I sell. Which reminds me, I need to get some cocoa to make chocolate muffins tomorrow."

"Oh, I can feel my waist expanding by just thinking about chocolate muffins," Annie said.

Alice laughed. "They're for a Devine Décor party over at Maplehurst Inn. Chocolate muffins are Linda Hunter's favorite. She's hosting a party mostly to get some discounts herself. She told me that she is planning to redecorate a couple of the rooms at the inn, just to spruce them up a little."

"Well, having stayed in one of those rooms, I found the decor lovely," Annie said.

"She's trying to get away from the farm country look to something a little French, I think," Alice said. "She wants something a little more upscale."

Annie sighed. She liked country, but she was glad Alice's work was doing so well in the difficult economy. It had certainly had its ups and downs in the past couple of years. As she sipped her coffee, her mind drifted to her worries about her family. She told Alice about LeeAnn's phone call.

"She must be worried sick," Alice said.

Annie nodded. "I offered to help out, of course, but LeeAnn said they're fine. They have savings, and Herb has a good severance package. I just hope he can find a new job quickly."

"Poor Herb," Alice said. "Job hunting is miserable."

"Especially these days." Annie shook off the gloom trying to settle in on her and forced a smile. "Speaking of jobs, I have a little one to occupy me for the next few days."

"Oh, what's that?" Alice asked.

"Ian asked me to look after Tartan for him." Annie explained about Ian's mother-in-law.

"Oh, sounds like Ian is in for some rough days," Alice said. "You know, my nana always said that bad luck comes in threes. Ian, LeeAnn ...." She raised her eyebrows.

Annie shook her head ruefully. "I don't believe in luck. Or superstitions."

"Still, makes me nervous to be your best friend," Alice teased. "Tell me, do I look pale?"

Annie truly didn't believe in such superstitious talk, but she still enjoyed Alice's teasing. She glanced up at the clock on the wall and yelped, "Time to go!"

They put their coffee mugs in the sink and hurried out the door for church. "Do you want to take separate cars?" Alice asked as they crossed the porch.

"We'd better since I have to go to Ian's as soon as the service is over. I promised Tartan a walk."

"I could come with you," Alice said. "It would give us more time to chat."

With that decided, they chose Annie's car. Neither wanted to arrive at church with tangled hair, and a convertible with the top up was no fun at all. At least, that was Alice's view.

As Alice and Annie walked down the aisle at church, Annie smiled and nodded to several people. She found an empty pew and sat down, leaving a space for Alice at the end. She folded her hands in her lap, much as she had in this very church on the summer Sundays of her childhood. Then, as now, Annie enjoyed looking around the sanctuary, seeing the lovely clothes on the ladies, and feeling the warm sense of being surrounded by people who loved God.

Annie began idly naming the people she knew as she caught sight of them. She was surprised to realize there were whole rows where she knew every person on the pew. *I'm really not the new girl in town anymore*, she thought. Stony Point was home now as surely as Brookfield, Texas, had been. Brookfield held all the good memories of being in love, being married, raising LeeAnn, and then seeing her daughter start her own family. But Stony Point held memories of her grandparents, and she was building new memories with her close friends.

"I'm truly blessed," she said softly.

Alice turned to look at her. "Did you say something?"

"Just thinking out loud about how much I like living here," Annie said.

Alice nodded. "I had some trouble fitting back in here after my divorce," she said quietly. "But then Betsy made me realize that it wasn't the town closing me out—it was me closing them out. Now, I can't imagine being any-where else."

Annie nodded and then sat up straighter as the organist walked out in a crisp white dress with a beautiful cutwork hem and took her seat. Soon the rich sounds of the organ poured over the congregation. Annie took one more glance around the room and was somewhat startled when she spotted Adam Smithfield slip into a seat near the back of the church.

She had forgotten about the sad-eyed man on the beach, and she felt a pang of guilt about his letter. She knew she had taken it back to Grey Gables, but she couldn't remember where she'd put it. She slipped her purse into her lap unobtrusively and checked inside. No, she hadn't put the envelope in there. *Where is it?* she thought. She didn't remember seeing it since she'd brought it home.

She turned her attention sharply to the front as the choir director asked the congregation to open their hymnbooks. Annie picked up the burgundy-bound book and quickly flipped to the page, deciding she'd think about the letter later, and maybe the memory would come back to her. She let the beautiful hymn fill her with the warmth and comfort that she always found in spiritual music. For a mo-ment, she wished Ian was there sharing a hymnbook with her. She knew he could probably use a little comfort and peace today.

After the hymn, Reverend Wallace took the pulpit

and began with the weekly announcements. He reminded everyone about the upcoming church bazaar. "The proceeds from the bazaar will be going to the food pantry," he said. "I know we normally put the money into our Sunday school supplies, but we're still seeing such a need for the food pantry. So all the Sunday school teachers agreed to muddle along with last year's materials so that we could put the money toward the greater need."

Annie couldn't imagine what it must be like to have trouble feeding your family. She and Wayne had had some lean years leading up to the purchase of the car dealership, but they'd never struggled to put food on the table. And yet, she knew that was because they were blessed, not because they were especially worthy or more hardworking. Hard times could hit anyone, no matter how skilled or dedicated they were to their work. LeeAnn's call had suddenly made the financial struggles all over the country feel much more real for her.

"And finally, I want to thank the generous person who left us a tiny visitor this week. I have to admit, the children's minister and my wife are in some intense fellowship over whether this little beauty ends up in the Sunday school classrooms or at the parsonage." The Reverend's voice cut into Annie's thoughts, pulling her attention back to the front. He slipped a beautiful nee-dle-felted calico cat from the shelf inside the podium and held it up. The little cat was frozen in mid-step, and a tiny kitten dangled from her mouth. "The card left with this lovely sculpture is particularly appropriate to my message this morning." He held up the creamy paper that Annie recognized from the notes accompanying the previous sculptures and read aloud: "The Lord carries us when we are too small and weak to walk. So, too, do His people bear one another up. Thank you."

Annie blinked at the lovely sentiment as Reverend Wallace used it as a segue into his sermon on the church's duty to be a support to the small and the weak. Annie didn't know about everyone else, but she left the service with a renewed sense of the importance of being a servant and a support to others.

~ 9 ~

As they walked out of the sanctuary, Annie and Alice stopped several times to greet friends in the congregation. Finally they reached the sunny steps of the church. Alice turned to Annie and whispered, "That's the third of those sculptures I've heard about. Did you know Kate and Mary Beth found one at A Stitch in Time?"

Annie nodded. "I saw it."

"They're so beautiful," Alice said. "I am totally amazed to think we have someone in Stony Point who does work like that, and no one knows her."

"It could be a him," Annie said.

"It could," Alice agreed. "But I think more women are cat lovers and crafters."

Reverend Wallace spoke from behind them. "Are Stony Point's greatest detectives working on the case of the mystery cats?"

Annie turned, feeling her face flush, but Alice just said, "I think we are."

"Well, take care," the Reverend said. "We need to respect the person's right to give without the left hand knowing what the right has done. Matthew says there is a greater blessing when the gift giving is without applause."

Annie wasn't surprised to hear the reverend voicing the

very concern she'd had herself. It was difficult, though, to leave a mystery alone.

"Reverend Wallace?"

All three of them turned to face Adam Smithfield who smiled brightly. "I wanted to tell you how much I enjoyed the service." His eyes moved to Annie, and he nodded. "It's a pleasure to see you again, Mrs. Dawson."

Annie saw Alice look at her with one eyebrow raised, but merely smiled and greeted Adam. "How has your search been going?" she asked.

"Search?" Reverend Wallace echoed.

"I'm looking for a very dear friend," Adam said. "Candace Caine. I have reason to think she was in Stony Point at some time."

The reverend's brow wrinkled as he thought. "I know a Candace Wilson, but Wilson is her married name. She married Harry Wilson just two years ago. A wedding like that reminds us all of the timelessness of love. At any rate, is your friend in her upper sixties?"

Adam shook his head. "No, she's only about Mrs. Dawson's age."

"Oh, it's not Candace Wilson, then. I definitely don't know anyone else named Candace," Reverend Wallace said. "Though, not all tourists come to church, so she could have spent time in Stony Point without my getting to meet her."

"Candace would have come to church," Adam said. "She was very spiritually minded when I knew her. I don't think she'd miss church, not even when traveling."

"Did you come all the way to America to find this woman?" Alice asked.

"I did," the tall Brit said, "and I would go much farther."

"She must be very important to you," Alice said, and Annie could see the curiosity in her friend's eyes.

"She is the love of my life," Adam said simply; then he turned his attention back to Reverend Wallace when he asked what part of the United Kingdom Adam was from. "Cardiff, Wales," Adam said. "Though I live in London now."

"That's an amazing coincidence," Reverend Wallace said. "My wife's family has roots in Cardiff, and she still has many relatives living there that she keeps in contact with. I've only been once, but I really enjoyed the trip. Wales is a lovely place. I've always thought of New England as a region with a sense of antiquity, but Wales reminded me of what a young country the United States truly is. Wales felt ancient—especially in the countryside."

Adam smiled. "That reminds me of a joke. Do you know the difference between Americans and Europeans?"

"No, what's the difference?"

"In Europe, a hundred miles is a long way," Adam said. "And in America, a hundred years is a long time."

The group chuckled for a moment. Adam thanked Reverend Wallace again for a fine service and began to walk down the wide church steps. Annie walked after him and touched his arm. When he turned, she told him about finding the letter in the parking lot after meeting him on the beach.

"Oh, I'm so glad you found it," Adam said. "I was afraid that I'd lost it forever."

"I'm just sorry I didn't bring it to you before," she said. "I'm not sure where it is, though I know I brought it home with me. I'll look around my house and bring it to you at the inn."

Adam smiled, speaking tentatively. "Would you mind if I came home with you now and helped you look for it? You really don't know how panicked I was over losing it."

By this time, Alice had joined them on the steps. "Is it a valuable document?"

Adam's smile expanded to include her. "Not so much valuable in money terms, but it's definitely valuable to me. It's a letter from Candace, and it's the way I knew she was here at some point."

"Because of the postmark," Annie said. "The return address was New York City, but the postmark was here in Stony Point."

Adam looked at her in surprise. "That's right. You're very observant."

"Well ..." Annie said, hesitantly. She felt a strong desire to help Adam; she could tell he was desperate to find Candace. But she also remembered times in the past when strangers to Stony Point weren't as sincere as they seemed. Still, he wasn't being pushy. "Alice and I were going to a friend's house to walk his dog, but if Alice doesn't mind, we could go to my house first so I can search for the letter."

"That's not a problem," Alice said. "I have plenty of time."

So Alice and Annie piled into Annie's car and Adam followed in his rental. "You didn't tell me you met a handsome stranger—and with a gorgeous accent no less. As jealous as Ian gets, it's a good thing he's out of town."

"Ian doesn't get jealous," Annie said. "He's a little

overly protective of everyone in Stony Point. It's just part of being mayor."

"Right, sure," Alice said. "I can definitely tell you that he never acted quite so ... protective ... before you moved to town, Annie."

"Well, even if I were in the market for handsome strangers," Annie said, pulling the topic away from Ian, "which I am not, Adam clearly is solely focused on this Candace Caine."

"Why does that name sound familiar?" Alice asked.

"She writes children's books," Annie said. "I know the twins have at least one of hers."

"I guess that could be it," Alice said. "Not that I buy a lot of children's books. Did you hear him say she is the love of his life? I think that's so romantic. Did he tell you what happened?"

"He hasn't said, but he seems so sad about it."

"Maybe he'll tell you more while you two look for the letter," Alice suggested. "How exciting and mysterious. Do you think we could help him find her?"

"I don't know," Annie said. "The last time I tried to help a man who seemed to be mourning a lost love, it turned out that she had a very good reason to be hiding from him."

"You don't think Adam is dangerous, do you? He seems so genuine. If you think he might be dangerous, why are you letting him come home with you?"

"Well, he asked right in front of you," Annie said. "So I assume he's not planning to get me alone at Grey Gables and bash in my head. Besides, if he acts the least bit twitchy, I'll sic Boots on him. You know how protective she is."

"Probably more than Ian, that's for sure," Alice said. "More than one person can testify to that. I think Jim is truly scared of her."

"I think he just doesn't like cats," Annie said. "By the way, has Nancy Breaker asked you about putting the carriage house on the Garden Club's tour of homes?"

Alice shook her head. "I don't know what that is."

Annie explained about the pushy woman and her almost endless pestering phone calls. "I'm thinking I need to tell her a very firm 'no,' so she'll leave me alone. The other day I even had someone drive by, taking photos of the house."

"Are you sure that was about the tour?" Alice asked, a worried frown on her face.

"I can't imagine what else it could be about," Annie said. "But now I can worry about that, thank you very much. I needed some fresh worries."

"Anything to help." Alice leaned forward for a better view out the windshield. "Well, we should probably focus on the mystery at hand since we're almost home, and the tall, dark stranger is behind us."

Annie glanced at her friend and smiled mischievously. "Good thing I have you to protect me. Besides, I don't think Adam is at all dangerous, though I am not always the best judge of character. He seems so sad. Anyway, I'm sure it'll only take a few minutes to find the letter."

"This will give us a chance to change clothes before we walk Tartan. I've seen that dog. I think I'm going to put on my gardening pants since they're already grass-stained for Tartan's convenience."

Annie laughed. "That sounds like a good plan."

~ 10 ~

When Annie pulled into the drive at Grey Gables, Alice turned and looked behind them at Adam Smithfield's car. She raised an eyebrow and asked, "Do you want me to come in with you?"

Annie shook her head. "I'll be fine. Since he didn't try to make a secret of his coming with me, it's not likely he's planning anything unpleasant. I'm sure he just wants his letter."

"If you say so," Alice agreed.

Adam's car pulled in behind Annie's. Alice got out and walked past Adam on the driveway instead of cutting across the grass. "Nice to meet you," she said to him.

"It was a pleasure," he assured her.

Alice turned and waved to Annie. "I'll be over as soon as I change. Don't let Boots claw his face off."

Annie almost laughed again. Alice was certainly doing her part to send Adam a message that Annie wasn't alone. She waited a moment at the foot of the porch steps for him to catch up with her.

"You have a lovely home," he said. "I love Victorian architecture."

"It was my grandparent's home," Annie said. "I've always loved it. Oh, I should warn you. I have a cat, and she can be a little suspicious of strangers."

"Would this be the terrifying Boots?" he asked with a grin. "At least I now know what might claw my face off. Well, other than your friend Alice, who seems quite protective herself."

"Alice doesn't have claws."

"I wouldn't be completely sure of that," he said.

Annie opened the door, and they walked in just as Boots padded into view. Normally Boots would take one look at a stranger and puff up into an offended ball of fur and hiss. This time, she stopped and stared at Adam in frozen silence.

Adam knelt down and spoke quietly to the cat. He held out his hand. Annie tensed since she knew Boots could be quick with the claws. Instead, the gray cat sniffed his hand delicately and then rubbed her head against it. Adam scratched her ears.

"Now, that's a surprise," Annie said. "I've rarely seen Boots show such an instant fondness for anyone. She tends to be much more territorial than that."

"I love cats," he said. "Maybe she can tell. I haven't had one in years, though. When Candace lived in London, she adopted a cranky old black tomcat named Ebenezer. I would sneak him bits of fish and chips every time I visited her flat. He thought I was Father Christmas, I believe. When she left so suddenly, all she left me was a note and Ebenezer. The old cat and I consoled one another, I suppose. I haven't thought of old Ebenezer in years."

Adam stood, and Annie felt another pang of sympathy for the sadness that seemed to radiate from the tall man. She didn't know what to say, so she turned and tapped her chin in thought. "I know I was carrying your letter when I came in that day."

"And Boots probably greeted you," Adam suggested. "She seems like she would."

"Right, she was being very insistent about trying to trip me. I even had to put her in the mudroom so I could take a phone call." Annie's eyes opened wide. "A *phone call*. The phone was ringing when I came in."

Annie hurried into the living room and walked to the phone table. It was bare except for the phone. "Oh, I thought for sure it would be here."

She and Adam stepped back from the table and slowly circled it. Adam yelped in surprise and swooped down to pick up the envelope from where it lay wedged between the leg of the table and the side of the chair where Annie often sat as she talked on the phone. "Found it!"

"Oh, I'm so glad," Annie said. "I remember now. Boots was marching around on the table. She must have knocked the letter off."

"Old Ebenezer was the same way," Adam said. "He had a special fondness for running off with my car keys. Cats— they add so much insanity to your life."

"The letter looks old," Annie said. "Why are you only now looking for Candace in Stony Point?"

"Good eye," Adam said as he nodded. "I've carried it around for a couple of years. I had hired a private inves- tigator to help find Candace once I felt certain she was in America, but all the detective gave me was itemized bills, so I finally decided to search on my own."

"This is a long way to come," Annie said.

"I would travel much farther if I thought it would lead me to Candace. But no one I've spoken to seems to have ever met her." He sighed. "My company continues to publish her books, but they arrive from all different locations as if she's traveling the world. The handwriting on the packages is never hers. The handwriting on this envelope isn't hers either. We have an email address for editorial discussions, but we've not been able to trace it to any specific place. The only piece of evidence I have with her actual handwriting is the letter inside."

"Was that business correspondence too?" Annie asked.

He shook his head. "No, it was private—a letter asking me to quit looking for her. I have traveled to a few of the spots around the world where her packages originated. She must have heard about it."

"It sounds as though she doesn't want to be found."

"I'm sure she feels she has good reason for that. Things didn't end with us as I would have wished," he said as he tapped the letter gently against his hand. "But there are things she doesn't know. Things she didn't know then, and things that have changed since."

"Couldn't you write them to her?" Annie asked. "You said you have an email address."

"Some things can really only be said face-to-face." He sighed. "I'm not certain she would believe me otherwise."

Annie frowned slightly. She felt bad for the deep sadness that seemed to surround Adam, but she also believed a person had a right to privacy. Clearly Candace Caine didn't want to talk to him, and it was clear that she knew where to find him if she changed her mind.

Finally Adam smiled. "Thank you for keeping this letter safe. I appreciate it more than you know." As he spoke,

Boots jumped up onto the small telephone table, and he scratched the cat gently under the chin. "Nice to meet you too, Boots."

Annie saw Adam out the door and then hurried to her room to change into jeans and a sweater so she could walk Tartan. Minutes later, she was crossing the lawn that separated her house from Alice's. She saw Alice standing on the front porch of the carriage house, waiting for her.

"I decided not to intrude on your conversation with the mysterious stranger. I didn't want to interrupt, but I hope you're going to spill all the details now," Alice said. "So did you learn more about him and his mysterious writer?"

Annie shook her head. "Not much more than we knew before, really. I know he's looking for Candace Caine, and she doesn't want him to find her. Apparently they had some kind of horrendous misunderstanding."

"Failed romance," Alice said. "Probably his fault."

"What makes you think that?" Annie asked, even though she'd had a similar thought.

"He has that dark brooding look of a man who blew it and knows it," Alice said. "Guilty."

"You think so? I thought he just looked sad. But I don't think I'm comfortable with joining in a search for a woman who doesn't want to be found."

"I know I wasn't exactly thrilled when my ex turned up here in Stony Point," Alice said. "Though Adam doesn't seem like the same sort of man as John."

"Not really," Annie said, casting a sympathetic look toward Alice. Alice had married John MacFarlane after being swept away by his good looks and charm.

Unfortunately, John was a bit of a con man, and he certainly made Alice miserable.

Soon they pulled up the long driveway to Ian's house. Annie let them in with the key Ian had given her. As they started down the long hall from the front door, Alice darted into the cozy study.

"Alice!" Annie scolded. "Tartan is in the backyard."

"I just wanted to see if Ian had made any changes in here," Alice said. "The new Devine Décor catalog has some great masculine pieces, and I wanted to be able to suggest where they might go—if Ian is interested." Alice's eyes swept the room, and she pulled a notebook from her purse to write something down.

Annie just shook her head as she stood in the doorway. She actually liked looking at Ian's study too. It was such a perfect reflection of Ian's personality—flawlessly neat and organized, while still looking comfortable.

Alice looked over Ian's mantel and turned to look at Annie. "He certainly has put a lot of photos of Arianna out."

Annie reluctantly walked over and looked at the lovely, laughing woman in the photos. "She was very beautiful," she said softly. "I don't see any reason he shouldn't have photos of her."

Alice raised a shoulder. "You don't line your mantel with photos of Wayne."

Annie winced. "I still feel ambushed sometimes when I see a photo of him. That's when the sadness sneaks up on me. It's getting better though. I have a photo on my dresser of LeeAnn, Wayne, and me." Then Annie smiled. "Plus, the twins take up a lot of my photo space."

"I can understand that," Alice said. "They're adorable."

"Don't let John hear you say that," Annie said. "He likes to think of himself as manly and tough."

They laughed at the idea of the adorable little boy looking tough. Then they heard a sharp bark from outside. "It sounds like Tartan is ready for his walk!" Annie said.

Tartan was dancing with joy when they got to him, and Annie was glad she had Alice's help to hold the dog's collar while she snapped on the leash. He launched himself out of the dog run. Annie and Alice were soon trotting along behind him, laughing at the cheerful dog's antics.

The gallop around Ian's neighborhood left Annie and Alice pink-cheeked and breathless from laughing. "I can certainly see why Ian finds Tartan such good company," Alice said. "It would be hard to be depressed around that little clown."

"That's true," Annie agreed as she rubbed Tartan's ears while he wagged his stubby tail enthusiastically.

Annie repeated her neighborhood dash with Tartan on Sunday evening and twice on Monday. She thought the peppy schnauzer might calm down a bit when he got used to Annie's visits, but she didn't see any sign of that. *No wonder Ian stays so fit,* Annie thought on Monday evening when she brought Tartan back from a particularly long walk. She'd been trying to wear the dog out, but he had definitely outlasted her.

Annie got home to a ringing phone again, but she didn't have to battle Boots to reach the phone table this time. The cat was giving Annie the cold shoulder since Annie had started coming home smelling of dog.

Annie picked up the phone tentatively, hoping it wasn't another pushy call from the Garden Club woman. "Hello?"

"Mom," LeeAnn said. "You've certainly been out a lot."

"Dog walking," Annie said. "You could call my cellphone, you know. I usually have it with me."

"I know, but I wanted to chat when you were sitting down," LeeAnn said. "I have an idea and wanted to run it by you."

"What idea is that?"

"Well, Herb has been job hunting already, but I'm thinking this would be a great time for us to just pick up and move."

"Move?" Annie echoed.

"Yes—to Stony Point," LeeAnn said, her voice rising in excitement. "The kids love Stony Point when we visit. And they'd get to grow up with you. Plus, I'm ready for a little less rush in our lives."

"Well," Annie said tentatively. "You know I'd love to have y'all here, but I don't know that the job market is any better in Maine than in Texas. In fact, I suspect it's probably worse. Just this past Sunday, Reverend Wallace was telling us the food pantry here is still getting a lot of use from out-of-work families."

"Well, we might not be able to live exactly *in* Stony Point," LeeAnn conceded. "Herb would probably need to work in a bigger city, but that would still let us see you on weekends whenever we wanted."

"What does Herb think of this idea?" Annie asked.

"I haven't mentioned it to him," LeeAnn said. "I'm trying to decide on the best approach. Herb is not a big fan of change, but I think he'd really love Maine once he got there. And I have his resumé. I could send a few out to companies in Maine. Herb will like the idea a lot more if there's a job offer there."

"Hmmm," Annie said. "Do you remember the time I bought a new living room set without telling your dad? I thought it would be a fun surprise. So I rearranged the living room while he was at work and put in the new furniture. Do you remember?"

"Yeah," LeeAnn said, chuckling. "Dad hated it. He didn't want to tell you just how much he hated it, but he sat on the furniture like he was visiting the queen. Poor Dad."

"Yes. And since I'd bought the furniture in a close-out sale, I couldn't take it back. We just had to live with it. But it took your dad a long time to feel comfortable in his own home. I was unfair to him, even though I didn't mean to be, and he ended up feeling forced to accept something he really didn't like at all."

"And there's a message in there for me." LeeAnn said wryly.

"No one likes to feel bullied," Annie said. "Talk to Herb and listen to what he has to say. Be sure the whole family is on the same page. It's not just Herb; the twins will need to have a voice in this as well. New school, new friends—it's a lot for eight-year-olds to absorb. A whole new part of the country is much more drastic than new furniture."

LeeAnn sighed. "OK. Message received. But you know I'd love us to move up there, so I'm not totally giving up. Stony Point just feels like such a nice place to raise children."

"It is," Annie said. "And I would love to have you here. But don't forget we have a lot more winter here."

"That is a drawback," LeeAnn said. "Brrrr. I might have to take up quilting so I could pile thick quilts on all our beds."

Annie couldn't quite picture her high-energy daughter settling in one place long enough to piece a quilt, but she suspected she'd rained on LeeAnn's parade enough for one day. "Whatever you and Herb decide, just be careful. Moving is a pretty drastic decision after the shock of a job loss."

From there the conversation drifted to the twins and their spring activities. By the time they ended the conversation, Annie felt a little less worried. Still, she knew LeeAnn could definitely be a "full steam ahead" person when she saw something she really wanted. She hoped this whole idea didn't put a strain on their marriage.

Annie looked over at Boots, who sat on the sofa casting reproachful glances her way. "I don't suppose you'd be open to a comforting hug?" Annie asked, opening her hands to invite the cat into her lap. Boots just hopped down from the sofa and stalked out of the room.

$$\sim 11 \sim$$

On Tuesday, Annie settled into her chair at the Hook and Needle Club meeting with a sigh. She'd tried to get started on John's monkey cap, but quickly found herself confused about the color changes. She hoped Kate had time to help her. She was pretty sure she'd need to write minute instructions about the color changes right in the pattern book to keep them straight.

Stella looked up from her knitting and nodded at Annie. As usual, she had arrived for the club meeting well ahead of anyone else. "How are you coming with your caps for the twins?"

"I finished Joanna's cap," Annie said. She pulled the puppy cap out of the bag and held it up.

"That's very cute," Stella said approvingly. "I'm certain your granddaughter will love it."

"I hope so," Annie said. "I'm hoping Kate can help me sort out the color changes for the monkey cap."

"Color changing can be confusing," Stella said. "I remember I once did a sweater that had ten different colors. The pattern was very complicated. I do believe I gained some of my gray hairs from that one."

Annie laughed, grateful to the older woman for making her feel better. Annie often felt like the weakest crafter in the club, especially when she compared her work to the amazing knitting that Stella and Gwen could do—or even to the darling quilting and dainty cross-stitching that Peggy and Alice brought to every meeting. Even Mary Beth, who seemed to dabble in a bit of everything, amazed Annie with her versatility. And all of that was not to mention the work that Kate did on her beautiful creations.

The rest of the Hook and Needle Club arrived in a burst of cheerful conversation and smiles. Since the shop was *sans* customers, Mary Beth hurried over to take a seat of her own as soon as all the others were settled. "Let's start off with a mystery!" she said.

Peggy looked up so quickly from the quilt block she was sewing that her dark ponytail swung back and forth like a pendulum. "A mystery?"

Mary Beth nodded. "Most of you probably know that someone is leaving needle-felted cat sculptures around town."

Kate brought the small white cat sculpture from the counter, and they passed it around the group. "The workmanship is gorgeous," Gwen said.

Stella peered at the small cat's face. "This definitely demonstrates real artistic ability. Mary Beth, I would expect you'd know who in town works with wool roving. Where else would the artist get her supplies?"

"Not here," Mary Beth said. "I carry a few packages of wool roving and some needles. But I don't have more than the basic supplies for people who do small needle-felted accents like those flowers you did once, Stella. These cats definitely use colors I've never stocked."

"Oh, no," Alice said in mock horror. "Do you know what this means?" She paused for dramatic effect, and then she added in a whisper, "Someone in Stony Point is shopping at *another* craft store."

"Actually, the artist is probably buying online," Kate said. "When I need something Mary Beth doesn't have, she orders it for me. Of course, I'm here almost every day. This artist may simply be buying his or her things online because it's more convenient.

"Plus, it would tend to give away the person's secret if Mary Beth could name someone who ordered a bunch of cat-color wool roving through the store," Gwen added.

The rapid clicking of Stella's knitting needles paused as she said, "Since this secretive artist gave Mary Beth a sculpture, I think we can assume it's someone who must buy other supplies here. Otherwise, why would the person feel a sense of gratitude toward A Stitch in Time?"

"One thing is certain," Mary Beth said. "The person is skilled in more than one craft. We can see that with this little cat."

"I agree. This knitted pillow is lovely," Gwen said as she lightly stroked the soft pillow that the tiny cat sat on, "and the crochet on the pillow lace is extremely delicate. My guess would be that this isn't an elderly person. Working with fine thread like that requires better close vision than *I* have."

Stella sniffed. "The artist could have used a large magnifier. I sometimes use those to read the print in patterns. I would assume, however, that no one with arthritis could handle the fine thread."

"And it must be someone who likes cats," Alice said. "The only crafter I know who had made cats is Jane

Swenson. She made a kitten out of socks for her great-niece. I saw it. It was very cute."

"There's a big difference between a sock kitten and this kind of work," Stella said, gesturing toward the sculpture.

"True," Alice admitted. "Since we have no idea who does needle felting, maybe we should look at people capable of doing that kind of fine crochet and who also knit."

Peggy flashed a mischievous look toward Kate. "I know someone who crochets every bit that well and better."

Kate laughed. "I could make the lace. I don't knit, though I might manage a little square pillow like that. But I certainly could never do needle felting like that." Then she turned a smile on Stella. "Stella did those needle-felted flowers, and she is an amazing knitter. Do you have skills you haven't shared with us?"

"My efforts at needle felting merely taught me that my real gift is knitting," Stella said. "And I do very little crocheting. I wouldn't tackle such a complicated pattern as the one used for that lace."

"That brings us back to you, Mary Beth," Alice said. "Do you know who could crochet with fine thread like that?"

"Well, present company excluded," Mary Beth said, "I know that Taylor from the teen crafting group is really into amigurumi these days, so her crochet skills are getting stronger and stronger. She's certainly young enough to work with fine thread, even though I've never sold her any. And then there's Nancy from the Garden Club. She works with some fine thread with those endless doilies that she makes."

"I've seen a few of those at the church bazaars," Stella said. "For a tiresome woman, she certainly does some beautiful crochet." Stella groaned slightly as if she'd had a painful thought. "I suppose I could ask her about needle felting the next time she calls to annoy me about her tour of homes."

"And I could have Vanessa ask Taylor whether she's ever tried needle felting," Kate said. "She might talk more freely to another teenager, and you know my daughter loves being in on mysteries. Still, I think it would be highly unlikely that Taylor has secretly reached that level of skill. The sculpting in that cat is amazing. Every time I look at it, I expect the little thing to move."

"We need a place to start," Mary Beth said. "So I think you should let Vanessa ask."

"It might be a good idea if someone checks back at each venue that received a sculpture," Gwen said. "Clearly, the artist is someone who has an affection for the church, this shop, and the library. Maybe we could look at people who have that in common."

"And we can eliminate virtually all the tourists," Alice said. "We're still so early in spring that hardly anyone with a summer house has shown up yet. So it must be a resident."

"Someone who loves to read, craft, and go to church," Alice said with a chuckle. "That would include everyone here."

Mary Beth turned toward Annie. "You're awfully quiet in all this, Annie. Don't you have any theories? You have more mystery-solving experience than any of us."

"Reverend Wallace said he wasn't sure we should really pursue this mystery," Annie said, "because the person clearly wants to remain anonymous."

"With the few clues we have to go on," Gwen said, "the person is likely to stay anonymous as long as he or she wants. Still, the fun is in trying."

"I guess," Annie said.

"At least we can be certain *this* person isn't up to something nefarious," Stella said. "I can't see any way these little cats could be the focal point for some crime wave."

"If we figure out who the artist is, we'll keep the secret," Mary Beth said. "Won't we?"

Everyone agreed, but Annie already knew how good her friends were at keeping secrets. Between them all, anything that went on in town became common knowledge in hours.

"Annie and I can take a simple task that doesn't involve prying into anyone's secrets," Alice said. "We'll take photos of all the cats. That way we can compare them and see if there is any obvious clue in how they're made."

"OK," Kate said. "Mary Beth and I will brainstorm a list of people who could do the knitting and crocheting we see in the cat's pillow."

"I think we're overlooking a task," Stella said.

Everyone turned to look at her. "What's that?" Mary Beth asked.

"We know about the cats found in places we frequent," Stella said. "But how do we know if we're aware of all of them? I believe we need to ask at all the businesses in town."

"Good idea," Gwen said. "I'll help."

Mary Beth rubbed her hands together happily. "Then the Hook and Needle Club is officially on the case. This mystery doesn't stand a chance."

— 12 —

Since everyone in the club now had a task to accomplish in an attempt to solve the mystery, the group turned to talk of the church bazaar. Everyone began pulling small items from their project bags to donate to the bazaar. Mary Beth fetched a box from the back room for the items.

"This little bunny purse is so sweet. I would have loved something like that as a child," Gwen said as Annie passed her donations toward the box. "And these little belled toys are adorable."

"Boots thought so," Annie said and then told them about having to fish the cat out of the project bag repeatedly.

"So maybe they need to be advertised as cat toys," Gwen said. "Since they have the Boots seal of approval."

Annie was happy to see that the box was soon brimming with items. Since her little toys were so small, she'd worried that she wasn't doing enough. Once Mary Beth had gathered all the bazaar items, the group gradually broke up, chatting about the mystery as they left the shop in small groups. Annie smiled as she watched Gwen and Stella leave, their heads close together as they talked about possible suspects for the mystery artist. Her friends certainly loved mysteries.

"Shall we head out to start our photo shoot?" Alice asked.

"If you don't mind waiting for a few minutes," Annie said, "I'm desperate to get some help with my monkey cap from Kate."

"No problem," Alice said. "I'll take some pictures of the shop cat first."

Kate switched chairs to sit beside Annie and looked over Annie's attempt at the cap. "Oh, you're not off by much," she said encouragingly as she pointed out the problem.

"I knew I was off, but you spotted it so quickly. Could you write the changes on the pattern? I'm clearly horrible at remembering." Annie pulled out the pattern book, and Kate wrote in the color changes in small neat letters.

By the time Kate was done helping Annie, Alice was at the front counter clowning around about her photo shoot of the small sculpture. She used her cellphone to snap pictures of the cat and the card, all the while pretending to be a fashion photographer. "Give me more passion, darling," she cooed at the little cat.

"You certainly enjoy your work," Annie said as she joined her friend.

"Why do something ordinary when you can do it silly?" Alice asked. She slipped her phone back into the pocket of her floral blazer, and they set off to the library for the next photo shoot. "You're very pensive today, Annie. Are the good Reverend's words really weighing on you that heavily?"

The spring breeze seemed to wind-tunnel up Main Street, tossing Annie's fine blond hair into her eyes. "Yes and no," Annie said as she fished in her purse for a hair band and pulled her hair into a ponytail. "I do want to be sure we don't hurt someone with our curiosity. Mostly though, I've been worrying about LeeAnn."

"You mean with Herb losing his job?" Alice asked.

"Again, yes and no." Annie told her about LeeAnn's plan to move to Stony Point.

"I'm surprised you don't jump at the idea of having LeeAnn and the kids around," Alice said. "I know you miss them."

"I do," Annie agreed. "But I know that if the whole family isn't happy, eventually no one is happy. LeeAnn can be very strong-willed, and I am not sure she's communicating very well with Herb right now."

"Ah—another reason I'm just as glad I never had kids," Alice said. "Eventually you have to let them make their own mistakes while you worry and fret."

"I am trying to be objective, but I don't want LeeAnn to make a mistake that will hurt her family," Annie said. She smiled wryly. "As far as worrying and fretting, I'm guilty as charged."

They walked into the soft hush of the library, and Annie pulled her thoughts away from her family. Though she still wasn't certain it was fair to the artist to try to unearth his or her identity, she also had to admit that it seemed unlikely they'd manage it. The number of Stony Point residents who used the library, church, and needlework shop was fairly large.

"You know, something about this keeps bothering me," Annie said quietly. "Since A Stitch in Time didn't sell the materials for the sculpture, where did the materials come from? Why order supplies online when you can get Mary Beth to order them and save on the postage?"

"That's a good question," Alice said. "When I've needed items that Mary Beth doesn't stock, I've always just had her order them. But I guess if this artist didn't want anyone to know she did needle felting, she might have ordered for that reason."

"That would mean someone *learned* needle felting to this amazing level *just* to give mysterious gifts," Annie said. "Doesn't that feel a little unlikely?"

"So, do you have a theory about it?"

"What if the person leaving the cats isn't the one making them?" Annie asked. When Alice looked at her in surprise, Annie elaborated. "I would imagine a person could buy some lovely needle-felted sculptures online. Instead of ordering the supplies, what if the person giving the cats is actually ordering *cats*."

Alice nodded slowly. "I hadn't thought of that, but it makes sense. Maybe we should see what kinds of needle-felted sculptures are available online."

Annie and Alice walked quickly to the small bank of computers and signed in to share one. They settled in at the computer station with Alice sitting at the keyboard and Annie pulling up a chair alongside. Alice called up a search engine and typed in "needle-felted sculpture." Then they clicked on "Images" to limit the responses to just pictures. The screen filled with a gallery of beautiful needle-felted work. Many were animals, but they also saw a number of gnomes and fairies.

"If I spent much time looking at these," Alice said. "I think I'd feel an overwhelming urge to order a few myself."

"Do those images link to places to buy the pieces?" Annie asked. "It's one thing to find images, but another entirely to find a place to buy them."

Alice clicked on a lovely little orange cat lying on his back and stretching. The photo took them to an online shop where the artist sold her work. "So you could easily buy needle-felted cats. That means anyone could have left the cats. The actual cat artist didn't have to come from around here."

"Except that our cat included a book from our library sale." When the voice spoke behind them, Annie and Alice turned in their chairs to see Josephine Booth. "That would certainly suggest that the person who made the cat lives around here." Josephine peered at the screen from behind them. "Though that is a pretty little cat too. Still, I like ours better."

"Maybe someone bought the Cheshire Cat online and just added the book part himself," Alice said.

"I don't think so," Josephine said. "The cat is more than just sitting in the book. Come and look at it. You'll see what I mean."

The three women walked into the children's section and Josephine unlocked the glass case to take out the sculpture. "I've spent a lot of time looking at this little guy. Look at the size ticket in his hat," she said. "It's actually cut from one of the John Tenniel illustrations of the Mad Hatter. So it came from the book that the cat is sitting in. And look closely at the cat's smile. His teeth are paper. They came from another illustration in the same book. And I know this book came from this library. I remember it clearly."

"I found something else." The quiet voice came from a slight young woman with a sweet smile who stood with a picture book clutched to her chest.

Josephine smiled at the young woman. "Annie, Alice, I don't know if you've met Sarah. She's helping out in the children's room. The kids love her story times."

Sarah blushed slightly at the compliment and seemed to hug the book she was carrying a little tighter. "Nice to meet you. I believe I saw your grandchildren in here some months ago."

"I remember them saying they enjoyed story time," Annie said. "I believe it featured pirates?"

"It might have," Sarah said. "Pirates are always a crowd pleaser."

"You said you found something?" Alice prompted.

"Oh yes. You need to see this book." Sarah opened the picture book she'd been carrying and held it out. "Do you see the little handwritten bits on these illustrations? It looks like the same handwriting as on the cards. Well, to me it does."

Annie peered at the illustration. It was a photo of a soft collage made from bits of fabric and tufts of wool. The piece was embellished with buttons and beads and such, all very intricately combined to form a scene of a village. The little village shops had hand-lettered signs identifying them as the inn or the bakery. Annie looked from the card in the display case to the little signs. Though Annie was certain she'd never seen the picture book that Sarah held, something about the illustration looked very familiar. "The printing does look a lot alike."

"Who illustrated this book?" Alice asked. "It would be too much to ask for it to be someone from Stony Point."

Sarah shook her head, and then her blush deepened. "That's the only problem. I'm fairly certain this woman lives in England. All of her books are published there." She closed the book so they could see the cover. The author and illustrator were the same person: Candace Caine.

Annie and Alice looked at one another, wide-eyed. The woman that Adam Smithfield was searching for was the same person who was leaving cats around Stony Point!

"I know," Sarah said with a self-deprecating laugh, mistaking their stunned expression for surprise that she would advance such a silly theory. "It must just be a coincidence that the printing looks so similar."

"They certainly look identical," Josephine said. "It's a mistake anyone would make. It's amazing to think two people could have the same distinctive printing. Perhaps the artist is intentionally copying that writer."

"Actually, the answer might be even more amazing," Annie said. She told Sarah and Josephine about Adam Smithfield and his search for Candace Caine. "He has an envelope with a postmark from Stony Point, but this certainly makes it appear that Candace Caine did more than pass through Stony Point. If she's leaving these lovely little cat sculptures, she must live here or visit often, at least. You wouldn't go to this kind of trouble to thank people if you only passed through a town."

"I would certainly think we'd know if a world famous

children's author lived in Stony Point," Josephine said. "This woman has won some of the highest honors in children's book publishing in Great Britain. Her work is very famous."

"Apparently she's gone to a lot of effort to disappear," Annie said. "That would mean avoiding any actions that would make her presence here common knowledge."

Josephine sighed. "Well, if she is here, I wouldn't be surprised if she made the cats herself. The work she does in these books with collage is amazing. "

Sarah chimed in. "She does use a little needle-felting in the collages in some of the books from the last ten years. It isn't three-dimensional like the cat sculpture, of course, but that would be a logical next step in her skills. I could easily see the cats being created by Candace Caine. Her work is amazing." The young woman's admiration for the picture book illustrator was obvious in her voice.

"So we know she knows the technique," Annie added. Then she grinned. "It sounds like both of the mysteries have the same solution. Candace Caine is in Stony Point, and she's giving presents."

"We still don't know which of the ten thousand year-round residents of Stony Point is the famous Candace Caine," Alice said. "I know this is a major discovery, but I still feel just as much at square one on actually finding this artist as we ever were."

"Well, if someone moves to a whole new country and changes her name and hides this kind of talent from everyone in her new community," Josephine said, "she must be afraid of something. You don't go to that kind of effort just because you don't like publicity."

"What could a picture-book author have to be afraid of?" Alice asked.

Annie looked down at the perky grin on the cat in the display case. What had made his creator so afraid? And what part did Adam Smithfield play in that fear?

～ 13 ～

After taking a number of photos of the library cat and the card that came with it, Annie and Alice headed to The Cup & Saucer for lunch and a discussion of what they should do next.

Because it was midafternoon, the diner was mostly empty. As soon as they stepped through the door to the diner, Peggy rushed to them, her eyes shining with excitement. "You'll never guess what we found in the window near one of the tables!"

"A really big tip?" Alice said.

"A cat sculpture!" Peggy said, and she tugged them toward the hostess stand. She reached into the back of the shelf behind the menus and pulled out a porcelain teacup. Inside the delicate cup sat a saucy little tuxedo cat with a red bow tie around his neck. The needle-felted cat sat on a tea bag that lay in the bottom of the cup like a pillow. The string of the tea bag hung over the edge of the cup, and the oversized tea-bag tag read, "Always a Warm Welcome Here—Thanks!"

Annie recognized the printing. It matched all the other cards as well as the print from the picture book they'd looked at in the library.

"Isn't he adorable?" Peggy gushed. "I'm just so thrilled that we got one. I swear Jeff is treating it like an award."

"I would too," Alice said. "After all, all these little cats seem to be someone's way of saying 'thank you' for all the good things in Stony Point. It's nice to be one of the good things."

"That's how I feel too," Peggy said. "I wish I could take this little darling home with me. He's a charmer. Do you guys want to take his picture?"

Alice pulled out her phone and snapped a few pictures of the cat and the tag. "Did you happen to notice who sat at the table closest to where the cat popped up?"

"I've been going crazy trying to remember," Peggy said. She glanced toward the kitchen where a broad-shouldered man was glaring in her direction. "Oops, I better get you guys seated before the boss blows a gasket. Do you want a table or a booth?"

"Take us to the table nearest the cat discovery point," Alice said.

Peggy walked them to the front window. "Do you want lunch or just a snack? I have some wonderful strawberry pie. The strawberries aren't local, of course, but they taste great."

Alice grinned up at Peggy. "Sounds like a good day to have dessert for lunch," she said. "I'd like some strawberry pie with a cup of coffee, please."

"A small salad and tea," Annie said, smiling, "and then a piece of pie."

"Salad and pie?" Alice asked.

"The salad will make me feel virtuous."

Peggy dashed off to fill their order, and Alice looked at Annie, whose face had fallen back into a worried frown and asked, "We've found a major clue to two mysteries, so why do you look fretful instead of triumphant?"

"I don't like the way both mysteries are coming together," Annie said. "Now I don't know if I should tell Adam that the woman he's looking for definitely seems to be here in Stony Point somewhere."

"Maybe if we find her, we can ask her," Alice said. "We can let her decide whether to contact him." Alice leaned forward. "In fact, I think this means we have to find her."

"Maybe," Annie said. "I *would* like to tell her how sad he seems."

The women fell silent as Peggy brought their food. "This place was crazy this morning," she said. "I think you two must be the only people in Stony Point who *didn't* have breakfast with us. I know Addy from Dress to Impress sat here before she started work. She always sits where she can watch the shop."

"I don't think it's her," Annie said tentatively. If Candace Caine was the one leaving the cats, she was older than the young shop girl.

"Um, Liz Booth and Peter Warren had a late breakfast," Peggy said. "They sat here." She paused and wrinkled her brow. "Oh wait. No they didn't. They sat there." She gestured at the next table over and sighed. "Now I'm just confusing myself. I'll keep thinking about it though." Peggy turned as the door to the diner opened, and she hurried off to greet the three fishermen who stood inside.

"You know, it's amazing to me that Candace Caine has been here all along. John and Joanna have a book by her, and they love it." Then Annie's eyes opened wide. "You know, I found a couple picture books in the attic when I was bringing down all my grandfather's books. I couldn't decide whether to mail them to the twins or put them in the bookcase downstairs for the next time they visit, so I left them where they were for the time being. I believe they were Candace Caine books; in fact, I'm sure of it."

"Do you think looking at them would help?" Alice asked. "Though I imagine Adam has seen all those books—if there were clues in them, wouldn't he have noticed?"

"Probably," Annie agreed. "What interests me is that they were in the attic at all. They weren't mine. Adam said Candace Caine is only about my age, so the books weren't from my childhood. Why would Gram have picture books in the attic?"

"Maybe she was saving them to give to the twins as a gift?" Alice suggested.

"In the attic? They were in a trunk. If Gram wanted to send them to John and Joanna, wouldn't she keep them in her room or somewhere handy?"

Alice smiled. "Maybe she got them from Candace. Betsy seemed to know everyone and their secrets."

"Well, I hate to jump to conclusions, but I think I need to take a second look at those books," Annie said.

"A trip to the attic!" Alice said, her eyes sparkling. "May I come? You know how I love attic adventures. We always seem to bring down something that triggers all kinds of chaos."

"I don't know that I like looking at it that way," Annie said.

Alice shrugged. "I call them as I see them. So, when are we poking around the attic?"

Annie looked over Alice's lovely spring outfit of sage linen slacks and a cream sweater. "Are you sure you want to go attic adventuring in those clothes? I am trying to keep the dust down up there, but I've been so busy ...."

"I can change," Alice said, "and then come over. Oh, no, wait. I can't do it this afternoon either. I have a Devine Décor party tonight, and I promised to bring muffins, which I haven't even begun yet. You totally have to give me a rain check. You know how I love poking around for mysteries in the attic. I can come tomorrow."

"I think I can manage to hold off until then," Annie said. "I still have John's monkey cap to work on and a wild schnauzer to walk."

They finished up their snack and left money on the table, enough for food and tip. As they were heading toward the door, one of the fishermen called out to Alice. "Hello, pretty lady," he said. "I was going to call you."

Alice smiled at him. "Sure you were, Stan. What brings you guys in from fishing so early?"

"Storm coming," Stan said. "I don't think it's a big one, but the weather report was full of dire threats, so we decided it was big enough." He grinned, his eyes flashing. "Besides, we already had a decent haul, and we don't want to be working too hard."

One of the other men burst out laughing. "I don't think we have to worry about that too much with you!"

"Hey, now, you're making me look bad in front of my girl!"

"I'm not your girl," Alice said, "except maybe in your dreams."

This brought another burst of laughter, and Stan's eyes sparkled. "I'll spend the afternoon dreaming then!"

Alice just shook her head as the group laughed again. She and Annie wove though the rest of the tables and headed outside.

Annie looked fretfully up at the sky. "If it's going to storm, I need to go take Tartan on another walk right away and put him inside before the storm comes. Ian has a nice little doghouse in the run, but I'm sure he wouldn't want Tartan out in bad weather. The dog might even be afraid of storms. I know some dogs are."

"I probably need to put the top up on the convertible," Alice said with a sigh. "Have a good walk with Tartan. I'll head home and switch into baker mode. Do you want me to save you a muffin?"

"Do you ever actually have leftovers?" Annie asked incredulously.

"Not usually," Alice said, "but I could hide one."

"That's OK," Annie said. "You should use them to wow your customers. You'll sell a bunch once everyone is swooning over your baking."

"It doesn't hurt," Alice agreed.

Annie was soon on her way to Ian's. Tartan greeted her with the same enthusiasm he always showed. Since she'd had several days to practice, she managed to get his leash hooked on the first try. "I'm going to be a Tartan expert by the time Ian comes home," she said as Tartan danced around her.

They set off on a brisk walk, since Tartan didn't know how to have any other kind of walk, and Annie thought about the mysterious author as she and Tartan hurried along. She wondered what could bring someone to change her name and hide in a town far from home. She thought of her old friend, Susan, who had done nearly the same thing once, but Susan had an excellent reason for running—she was running for her life.

No matter how skeptical Annie tried to be, she just couldn't picture Adam Smithfield as the kind of controlling monster that had driven Susan to run away. Annie felt herself pulled back and forth about the mystery. Was she being nosy by helping track down a woman who didn't want to be found? On the other hand, curiosity was Annie's weakness. She had never been good at leaving things undone.

When she and Tartan finally got back to Ian's, Annie led the dog into the mudroom and unhooked his collar. Tartan scratched at the door that led to the kitchen and whined. "I know," Annie said. "I miss Ian too, but he's not in there. I hope he'll be home soon." She squatted down and stroked the dog's head. "I'm sure he misses you too." Tartan gave her a small lick on the end of her nose for her kindness.

When Annie headed for the back door, Tartan drooped a bit. "Oh, don't do that," Annie said. "If tomorrow is nice, I promise to take you for an extra walk on the beach right after Alice and I have our attic adventure. How about that?"

Tartan perked up at the word "walk," but then he flopped down with a sigh as Annie went on outside. Annie shook her head as she walked to her car. Pets certainly knew how to make a person feel guilty.

She made the drive home quickly and smiled to see Alice sitting on her front porch in one of the wicker rocking chairs. Alice stood up and waved as Annie passed by to pull into the driveway at Grey Gables.

Annie walked across the lawn to the carriage house, and Alice gestured at the chair beside her. As Annie sat down she saw that Alice was holding a kitchen timer. "I'm timing the muffins," Alice said. "Since I didn't get to ride home with the top down, I thought I'd sit on the porch and watch the storm coming."

"I don't think it's going to be as fierce as the fishermen made out," Annie said, "but I'll only sit for a minute so I don't get caught in it."

"How was your walk with Tartan?" Alice asked.

"Guilt producing," Annie said. "I promised him an extra walk tomorrow."

"You're such a pushover," Alice teased.

The timer in her hand went off with a shrill beeping, making both women jump. Alice headed in to tend to her muffins, and Annie walked home. She stopped to admire the pink buds all over the flowering almond bush at the edge of Alice's yard. She loved the dense pink blooms on the bush and wondered if she might find a spot somewhere in her yard for one.

Boots greeted her with a cold snub—Annie once again smelled of dog—and she found that cat's disapproval gave her several hours of uninterrupted crocheting on John's cap. The notations Kate had made on the pattern made the color changes for the cap much easier, and when Annie stopped to put the cap away and fix supper, she'd not had to pull out a single row.

~ 14 ~

The next morning, Annie hurried to Ian's at dawn to get in a quick walk with Tartan before Alice came over for their trip to the attic. The morning was foggy and threatened more rain later. As always, the dog greeted her with lavish affection. "I thought Boots made me feel good," Annie said as she snapped on his leash, "but you're like the whole welcome wagon stuffed into one furry body."

The fog still quietly covered the streets as they walked. It felt like a million tiny drops of icy rain against Annie's skin. She wondered if that was what it would feel like if you could walk in the clouds. "It would probably be even colder," she said aloud. Tartan look eagerly at her, and Annie stopped to pet his soft ears. "I'm afraid our beach walk might have to wait for another day, sweetie. It's looking a bit soggy today, and I'm going to have to put you back inside. I promise to race over and let you out if the weather clears up."

Not understanding a word she said, Tartan simply soaked up the attention with his usual boundless cheer.

When she finished the walk and drove home, Annie was surprised to see Alice already crossing the yard between them as she pulled in.

"I know," Alice said sheepishly. "I have no patience."

"That's not a problem," Annie said. "I don't need to

change since Tartan already decorated my pants with paw prints—so a little dust shouldn't be a big deal."

They stepped in the door, and Boots raced over to greet them. She took one sniff of Annie's slacks and immediately stalked past her to visit with Alice instead. "She has been pointedly ignoring me ever since Ian left," Annie said.

Alice scooped up the gray cat and gave her a hug. "You know you should make friends with Tartan," she said. "He may be your brother some day."

Annie laughed. "You have a vivid imagination. Ian and I are just really good friends."

"I don't know," Alice said. "Ian doesn't call me when he needs a dog sitter."

"He probably doesn't want to be teased endlessly," Annie said.

"Sure, sure, that's the reason," Alice said, and then she gestured toward the stairs. "Shall we head to the attic? I don't suppose we'll find the mystery up there this time, but we might find some clues."

"After you, Nancy Drew," Annie said.

They walked to the second floor with Alice still carrying Boots. The cat normally didn't like being carried, but Annie suspected Boots was just tolerating it to show she liked Alice better than Annie. Boots had made it very clear that the smell of dog on Annie marked her as a traitor.

When they reached the narrower attic stairs, Alice set the cat down. "These are steep enough without carrying you, Miss Tubby," she said.

Boot sat and began carefully smoothing all the fur that had gotten rumpled from being carried. "I'll be happy to have her stay down here," Annie said. "She's always jumping out from behind things up there. I do believe half my gray hairs are a direct result of that cat in the attic."

At the top of the stairs, Annie looked over the mostly neat rows of trunks and boxes in the attic. She was constantly amazed at how many people had entrusted their special things to Gram's care during her lifetime. The attic of Grey Gables was like the Smithsonian—it served as the storage place for many of Stony Point's secrets.

"You know, nearly every time I poke around up here, someone ends up mad at me," Annie said.

"That's the thing about secrets. Most people are afraid to see them exposed," Alice said, "but you've done a lot of good too. Sometimes things have to be uncovered if they have any chance of healing."

Annie nodded at that. She had made some close friends through uncovering mysteries from the attic too. She knew more about her family. And she helped some people stop being afraid all the time. "Do you suppose Candace feels like that?" Annie asked, expecting somehow that Alice could read her mind.

"Like what?" Alice asked, looking up from a box she'd been peeking in.

"Afraid all the time," Annie said.

"Well, I guess if you're running away from something, it does make you afraid." Alice ran a hand through her thick auburn hair. "I used to feel that way about John. I was scared half to death when he came here looking for me. I guess I was afraid I'd be stupid all over again."

"He can be very charming," Annie said. "And he's handsome."

"But now that I really know him, he doesn't seem so handsome or charming," Alice said. "I found out that I've definitely grown wiser." She looked around the attic. "So where are those books?"

"In a chest over here," Annie said, easing her way down a row. "I'm sure I put them in there." She opened the large steamer trunk and took out a tissue-wrapped bundle. When she unwrapped it, two picture books were revealed.

"Wow, they're in great shape," Alice said. "They look like new."

"Yeah, Gram didn't wrap a lot of books in tissue like this," Annie said. "I remember being surprised. But if she bought them for the twins, I guess I could understand that."

Alice took one of the books and began to flip through it. "Candace Caine made some beautiful collages for these books. You could look at them all day and discover something new on every page."

"That's probably what's made her books so popular," Annie said. "They really are works of art."

"Just like the cats," Alice said. She flipped to the title page and froze. She looked up at Annie and slowly held up the book so Annie could see the page. It was signed, "Thank you for Sanctuary, Candace Caine." The inscription was written in the same careful printing that they'd seen on the cards and tag included with the needle-felted cats.

"Well, I guess we know why Gram had the books," Annie said. "She knew Candace Caine!"

"We should take a photo of the handwriting," Alice said,

and she handed the book to Annie as she fished in her pocket for her cellphone. Annie held the book up for the photo, and a slip of paper fell out and fluttered to the floor.

Annie bent to retrieve it. "It's a form of some kind," she said, "but it's a little faded. We should take it downstairs where the light is better. It's from some place called 'Friends of St. Francis.'"

"I don't think I've heard of it," Alice said. "Do you suppose it's a church? Maybe some kind of church auxiliary group?"

Annie shrugged. "Maybe. Is there a church around here with St. Francis in the name?"

"Not that I know of," Alice admitted. "Maybe it was a church in London."

They carried the books and the piece of paper downstairs to the kitchen. Annie put the kettle on for tea, and they sat at the small table near the window while they waited for the pot to boil. Annie glanced out the window and saw the rain had started, though it was far from a scary storm. It seemed like a normal spring shower. Then she turned her eyes toward the faded paper.

"Oh," she said as she held the paper up turning it toward the light of the window. "The Friends of St. Francis was some kind of animal shelter. This is about the adoption of a kitten."

"Maybe it's Boots," Alice said. "What does it say about the kitten?"

"Health, shots, age—that sort of thing," Annie said. She held the paper closer to the window to get as much light on the cramped and faded print as possible. The kitten is described as gray with white stockings. It *must* be Boots!" Annie flipped the paper over, but the back was blank. "Why would Gram stick the adoption paper for Boots in a picture book?"

"Maybe she was using it for a bookmark," Alice suggested.

"Who needs a bookmark for a picture book?" Annie said. "They take about five minutes to read. You don't really need to take a break in the middle."

"It's a mystery," Alice said, dropping her voice to spooky tones. She turned to open one of the books and began flipping pages. "These really are gorgeous. Are you going to give them to the twins?"

Annie nodded. "Eventually." She took the other book and began slowly turning pages. The book told the story of a magical bookstore in the middle of a tree. In nearly every picture, a small black cat with a white bib chest peeked out from behind books or twined around stools. "I wonder if this cat is Ebenezer," Annie said.

"Ebenezer?" Alice echoed.

"Adam Smithfield said Candace had a black tomcat that she left behind in London when she disappeared," Annie said as she turned the book around. "And this story has a black cat on every page."

"She manages some amazing detail for such a tiny cat," Alice said as she leaned close, examining the book. "Look at the way it's stretching in that picture."

"You know, if Candace loved cats, maybe she was involved in helping Gram get Boots," Annie said. "Maybe that's why the paper was in the book. I wonder if the Friends of St. Francis are still around."

"You should ask Mary Beth," Alice said as she slipped her hand into her blazer pocket and pulled out her cellphone. She offered it to Annie. "Nothing much gets past her."

"Do you know the number?" Annie asked. "I've found I never memorize numbers now that I have a cellphone. They're just all on my contact list."

"Same here." Alice scrolled to it quickly on her contacts, and Annie took the phone. Kate picked up the phone at A Stitch in Time on the second ring. Annie asked for Mary Beth and chatted with Kate a moment while Mary Beth finished with a customer.

"Have you solved the mystery already?" Mary Beth asked when she took the phone.

"Actually it may be getting even more mysterious," Annie told her. "Did you hear about the cat found at the diner?"

"Peggy called on her first break," Mary Beth said. "I thought I might go by and see it when I close up this evening. Have you photographed all the cats yet?"

"We haven't been to the church yet, but I wanted to ask you something. Have you ever heard of the Friends of St. Francis? I think it was some kind of animal shelter."

"More of an animal rescue with foster homes," Mary Beth said. "It closed about five or six years ago when the lady who founded it passed away. She had put up most of the funding, and the group couldn't continue without her. They were nice people, very dedicated to the cause."

"I found a piece of paper in a book that looks like it might have been from Gram's adoption of Boots," Annie said. "It sounds like she came from there."

"She might have," Mary Beth said. "But I know for sure that Betsy didn't adopt Boots. She got the cat as a gift."

Annie felt a surge of excitement. "From whom?"

"I really don't remember," Mary Beth said. "It's possible I never knew. I'm not sure. Let me ask Kate; maybe she remembers."

As Annie waited, she quickly told Alice what Mary Beth had just said. "You know," Alice said, "now that you mention it, I do remember Betsy saying something about Boots being the best gift she ever got outside of her family. I'd forgotten that, but it was when Boots got really sick from eating some houseplant. Betsy was so glad she pulled through and was a little gushy about Boots for a couple weeks after that."

Mary Beth's voice in Annie's ear pulled her attention back to the phone. "Sorry, Annie," she said. "Kate doesn't remember either. You might ask Stella or Gwen."

"Do you know of anyone in town who might have worked with the Friends of St. Francis?" Annie asked. "Maybe they'd remember the adoption."

"You could ask Dr. Martin," Mary Beth said. "Her dad took over the veterinary practice around here from your grandfather, and then Janet took over from her dad. Either her dad or she must have handled the care for the animals at the Friends of St. Francis. They might know more."

Mary Beth offered to ask around a little and see if anyone remembered Betsy telling them who had given her the kitten. "That would be great," Annie said. "Thanks."

As she handed the phone back to Alice, Annie considered calling the veterinary clinic, but then she remembered it was Wednesday. The clinic was closed to everything but emergencies on Wednesdays since they were open on the weekends. "Mary Beth suggested asking Dr. Martin about Boots," she told Alice. "But it'll have to wait until tomorrow."

"So, should we run over to take pictures of the last cat at the church?" Alice asked. "I know the church secretary should be there for another hour or so. She might go to lunch after that. I need to take her a Divine Décor catalog anyway."

"Sounds good!"

The rain had lightened to a heavy mist, but it was still far from convertible weather, so they drove to the church in Annie's car. Just as they pulled into the church lot, the sky seemed to open up again, and rain pounded the car.

"Hmm," Alice said. "I think I'll just sit here for a few minutes."

"Afraid you'll melt?" Annie teased.

"Are you saying I'm sweet," Alice shot back, "or comparing me to the Wicked Witch of the West?"

Annie laughed. "Sweet, of course."

"Speaking of sweet," Alice asked, "when is Ian coming home?"

"Oh, that's an interesting transition. I don't actually know. He hasn't called. He must be having a difficult time. From what he told me, his mother-in-law doesn't even remember that Arianna died."

"That can't be easy," Alice said. "Must drag up a lot of memories."

"I'm sure it does."

"It's too bad you're not there," Alice said, looking away from Annie at the rain. "You could help him get through it."

"He clearly never considered having me along," Annie said. "I'll admit, sometimes I do think Ian and I might end up being more than friends, but now, here's a big emotional thing in his life, and he's comfortable going it alone. That tells me that he and I really *are* just friends."

Alice turned to look at her. "It could be that he thinks it might be uncomfortable having you with him as he attends his dying mother-in-law," Alice said, frankly. "Or maybe it's telling you that he doesn't think you're ready for it to be more. Asking you to come along would have been a big step. Maybe you need to talk to the poor guy a little and find out how you both feel."

"I don't know what to say," Annie said.

"Tell him how you feel."

"I don't know how I feel," Annie said. "Sometimes I feel like I would like there to be more between Ian and me. And then sometimes I like things just the way they are. And hanging over all of that are my feelings for Wayne. I love him, and I miss him." Annie's eyes began to mist.

"Do you think you can only love one man in a lifetime?" Alice asked. "Because I loved John until I figured out what he was, and I love Jim now—even though that's probably always going to be a relationship that never advances past where it is."

"At least you know Jim is crazy about you," Annie said.

Alice nodded. "And I suspect the same is true about Ian's feelings for you. We've seen enough evidence of it."

"I know he's fond of me."

"Annie, my dear friend, you really need to sort this out and see where the relationship is going."

"I don't know," Annie said, leaning back on the headrest and closing her eyes. "I don't want to mess things up. I like having Ian for a friend. What if talking about it ruins that?"

Alice shrugged. "I'd just be careful about how long I waited to be honest with yourself—and Ian."

Annie opened her eyes and saw with relief that the rain had let up again. "Looks like we can go in now."

Alice chuckled. "Saved by the weather."

"You know it," Annie mouthed as she hopped out of the car.

~ 15 ~

When they reached the secretary's office, Alice tapped on the door frame and smiled at the sweet-faced young woman who had taken over as church secretary when the previous secretary retired. "Alice!" Ellen Whitaker said. "How nice to see you."

"I wanted to drop off the latest Divine Décor catalog."

"Oh, I'm so glad," Ellen told her. Then she patted her flat tummy and spoke softly. "We need some ideas for changing our guest room to a nursery."

"Really?" Alice and Annie both cried out together and rushed over to hug and congratulate the pleasant young woman.

Ellen beamed and thanked them, and then her smile turned curious. "I'm sure the both of you didn't brave the rain just to bring me a catalog. Did you need anything else?"

"We were hoping for a closer look at the little cat sculpture," Alice said. "I want to take some photos of it."

Ellen stood and gestured toward the door. "Sure. You're welcome to see it. It's back in the youth minister's office right now. I'm sure she's gone to lunch, but I know she wouldn't mind if you looked at it. She's been showing it off for days."

They headed through the halls of the church, and when they reached the minister's office, Ellen tapped on the door, pausing a moment before opening it. The little needle-felted cat was frozen in mid-step on the middle of the huge maple desk that took up virtually all of the space in the room that was not allotted to bookshelves.

Alice began snapping photos of the cat from different angles as Annie turned to Ellen, "Who found the cat in the first place?"

"Actually, that would be me," Ellen said. "It was the oddest thing. I went back to the supply room to get a new toner cartridge for the laser printer, and I saw the little cat prancing across the first shelf inside the door. Isn't it the cutest thing you've ever seen?"

"A supply closet seems an odd place to leave a gift," Annie said. "You would think a visitor would leave it in the sanctuary somewhere."

"I know—right?" Ellen said. "The closet isn't even marked or anything, so you wouldn't know what it was unless you looked in."

"Or unless you knew your way around the church," Alice said as she turned from her picture taking. "Oh, I'm sure it's not anyone here," Ellen said. "Who would want to keep that kind of talent secret? I figure some visitor was looking for the office or the children's church area and just got lost. These halls can be very confusing."

"How many people do you think would know exactly where the supply room is?" Alice asked.

"Well, there's me, of course," Ellen said, "and Reverend Wallace and his wife, and the youth minister, and the folks who clean, and all the Sunday school teachers and helpers. Some of the older kids, if they're sent to fetch things during service. I almost forgot about the choir director and probably some of the other music people." She bit her lip lightly as she thought. "Oh, and there's Mary Beth, of course, because she and the other ladies are storing some of their stuff in there for the hand-bell choir. And the ministry and outreach groups, and all the people who've ever volunteered for the bazaars, because they always store things in there."

"So everyone in Stony Point knows where it is except Annie and me," Alice said.

Ellen giggled. "It does seem like a lot once you start really thinking about it. Still, I expect it was a visitor who just got lost. So, is there anything else I can do for you? I need to do some quick filing before I head home. Is it still raining out?"

"Off and on," Annie said.

"We'll head on out now," Alice said. "Call me if you want anything from the catalog. Or would you like to have a party? It's a nice way to get free hostess gifts."

Ellen's eyes lit up. "I'll think about it." She laughed again. "Especially now that I've figured out how many people I see every day right here at the church. I ought to be able to get quite a crowd for a party."

Annie and Alice wove through the halls until they reached the side door again. The rain had stopped completely, and Annie could see that the afternoon sun was trying to peek through the clouds. "Maybe it'll be a nice day tomorrow," she said.

Alice looked up. "That would be great. I'll spend it working on my flower beds. I saw your azaleas were full of buds."

"Yes. They really should be beautiful any day now,"

Annie said. "My favorite point in the spring is when the azaleas bloom. They remind me of my home in Brookfield, even though our azaleas there would be bloomed and past by now. Here we're still seeing crocuses and snowbells."

They chatted more about flowers and the differences between seasons in Maine and Texas on the way home. When Annie dropped Alice off at her house, her friend leaned in the car window and said, "Don't forget to call me immediately if you hear of any clues from Mary Beth. Oh, and do you want me to go to the vet with you tomorrow?"

"Only if you want to," Annie said. "Though it would have to be after lunch. I promised Tartan a beach run if the weather is nice."

"I would offer to go with you to the beach, but Ian's dog makes me tired," Alice said. "I only feel old when I'm around that schnauzer. I should be around the house tomorrow if you want to grab me before you check out the vet."

"Great," Annie said. "Thanks."

As soon as she dropped Alice off, she remembered that she'd left Tartan inside at Ian's, so she drove over to give the dog another short walk before putting him in the run for a couple of hours. "I'll be back soon," she told him, "and you'll get three walks today after all."

Annie spent the rest of the afternoon scouting around the yard at Grey Gables and making a list of projects she needed to tackle. All the plantings around the house had been overgrown and weedy when Annie inherited the well-loved Victorian. They'd been a constant rebuke to Annie, reminding her of how she'd been inattentive to her grandmother's failing health. Of course, Gram never complained in any of their many phone calls, Annie reminded herself.

The hours Annie had put into the yard in the last three years really showed, and Annie knew Gram would be proud of the way Grey Gables looked, inside and out. It was the comfortable family home Annie remembered from her childhood summers again.

As the afternoon drew into evening, Annie took Tartan for the promised third walk. They circled Ian's neighborhood twice at a fairly brisk pace so that Tartan could use up some of his energy before being shut up for the night. "I'll have to tell Ian what a good boy you've been," Annie told the dog when they got home. "I know you must be tired of me by now."

By the time she got home, Annie was glad for a chance to shower and curl up on the sofa to finish John's cap. Since she'd showered off her last encounter with Tartan, Boots even consented to sit in her lap for a while.

Annie read over the color-changing directions several times before they began to sink in, and she realized she still felt a little too restless to focus. She redoubled her effort to concentrate, but finally gave in and set the cap aside. She went to her room for her laptop. She brought it to the living room and set it on the sofa.

Once it had booted up, she did a Web search for "Friends of St. Francis." There was always a possibility that someone—maybe a past volunteer or someone who had gotten a pet from there—had posted information about the group. She found many groups related to St. Francis and animals, but nothing about the group she was looking for.

Finally, Boots began pawing the keyboard in a bid for attention, causing the computer's Web browser to shut down several times. Annie put the cat on the floor, only to have her hop back onto the table. Finally Annie gave in. Boots was definitely more stubborn. "OK, back to cuddling the cat," she said as she shut the computer and Boots became her new laptop. They sat together while Annie's mind raced over the scant clues she had so far, until the ringing telephone jolted her out of her reverie.

Annie stifled a yawn as she picked up and said, "Hello."

"Hi Mom," LeeAnn said. "Am I calling too late?"

"Of course not," Annie said, instantly alert. LeeAnn knew that Annie wasn't exactly a night owl, so if she called late, it was important. "Is something wrong?"

"Nothing major, so don't panic," LeeAnn said. "But John knocked a tooth out at the park today."

"Knocked a tooth out!" Annie repeated, alarmed.

"He fell off the climbing tower ladder," LeeAnn said, "because he was hanging from it like a pirate. Apparently his face smacked the rope ladder on the way down. At any rate, the dentist said he knocked the tooth out cleanly, and he's going to be fine. It was one of his last baby teeth, and it was loose already. You know how late he teethed, and they say the later a child teethes, the later he loses them."

"Still, it must have been scary for both of you," Annie said.

"It was," LeeAnn said. "I'd had Herb drop us at the park on the way to an interview because my car is still in the shop. The twins were off school for a teacher workday, and they were feeling a little cooped up. Anyway, when John fell, I had no way to get to the dentist, and his mouth was bleeding like crazy. Luckily there were two other moms there that I knew. One drove John and me to Dr. Mansfield's office, and the other stayed at the park with her little girl and Joanna so she could let Herb know when he showed up. I didn't want to call and interrupt his interview."

"I'm sure he would have understood," Annie said.

"That's what he said," LeeAnn agreed. "But I didn't want him to be worried and distracted in the interview. You know nothing is more important to him than the kids. I had mostly gotten the bleeding stopped by the time we got to the dentist's office. Dr. Mansfield took us right in and everything was fine."

Annie laughed. "Well, I'm glad it worked out OK."

"It did, and you know what?" LeeAnn asked. "I realized something from it. We had this minor crisis, and I had friends right there at the park and a dentist who has known the kids since they cut their first teeth. I guess I had taken our home here for granted. It's nice to be surrounded by people who you can count on."

"So does that mean you're not going to try to talk Herb into moving to Maine?" Annie asked.

"Pretty much," LeeAnn said, her voice sheepish. "I really was a little out of control there for a while."

"It's understandable," Annie said, stifling another sudden yawn.

"Oh, Mom, I'm keeping you up," LeeAnn said.

"No, no, I'm fine," Annie insisted, though another yawn suggested otherwise.

"Look, I'll call again soon," LeeAnn said. "I just wanted

you to know about John, and to know that I think we're going to be fine."

"I'm glad," Annie said. "I have faith that all of this will work out. I love you, LeeAnn. Give the twins and their daddy a hug for me."

"I love you too, Mom," LeeAnn said.

After she hung up the phone, Annie scooped up Boots and said, "Now that I know everything is going to be just fine, I think it's time we went to bed."

— 16 —

Thursday morning dawned bright and warm, so Annie picked up Tartan for the promised romp on the beach. She was surprised to find that the normally overactive dog sat quietly in the car and simply looked out the rolled-up window during the drive.

Annie snapped on Tartan's leash through a slightly cracked car door. She knew better than to give the little dog a chance to rush out; she'd never catch him.

As she crossed the parking lot, she spotted Adam Smithfield's rental car. She wasn't sure if she wanted to talk to him. She was never really good at keeping secrets, but she wasn't ready to let him know that Candace Caine was almost certainly in Stony Point and giving gifts all over town.

The storm was past, but its remnants made the waves higher and rougher than usual, not that Annie had any interest in getting out in the icy water. She barely braved wading in the hottest part of summer.

She breathed deeply, smelling salt air and a faint fishiness that just avoided being unpleasant. Tartan trotted along beside her, his nose to the sand. He was so caught up in the smells that he didn't spot the gathering of gulls on the sand ahead of them until they took flight. Tartan pulled at the leash, barking wildly at the big flapping birds.

"Sorry, Tartan," Annie said as she bent to pet him. "Even

if I let you off the leash, I don't think you could quite manage to fly."

Tartan gave a last small yip and returned to sniffing along the waterline. Now and then he sniffed a bit too close to the surf and had to stop to snort and sneeze salt water out of his nose.

As Annie and Tartan walked toward a tall rocky ridge that extended into the water, she saw Adam Smithfield standing on one of the rocks, his face turned toward the churning water. Tartan either caught Adam's scent or saw him, because he began barking excitedly and tugging Annie toward the rocks.

Adam looked down at them, and his lined face lit up in a smile. "Annie Dawson, you do keep popping up wherever I go."

"Not intentionally," Annie said. "Are you looking for something up there?"

Adam shook his head as he began to make his way down from the rocks in little hops from rock to rock. Despite his height and look of gawky awkwardness, he was surprisingly surefooted. He landed in the sand and bent to scratch Tartan's ears. "I find the rugged coastline restful," he said. "It's like seeing my way home. And since I've had quite a frustrating visit to your lovely town, I can use the restfulness."

"No progress on finding your friend?" Annie asked.

Adam shook his head. "And yet, despite that, I can practically feel her here. Do you believe in premonitions?"

"Not exactly," she said.

"I never did either," Adam said. "But it's almost like I'm about to run into her. When I walk into one of the shops here, I feel as if Candace just left. Of course, I suppose that could be wishful thinking from a rather foolish man."

"Can you tell me more about Candace Caine? My grand-children are big fans of her work."

"She would love to hear that," he said. "She always loved kids and animals. She filled her schedule with school and library visits so she could read to the children. She said it helped her keep her vision sharp." He sighed deeply. "I asked at the library. I thought for certain that if Candace were here, she'd have volunteered to do the library reading hour, but they have a young woman doing that."

"Yes, I've met her," Annie said.

"Of course, Candace was quite young when I saw her last, or she seemed so to me," he said, turning his gaze out to the surf again. "She was such a little thing, though a bit plumper than the terribly skinny American women one sees in the movies."

"The movies aren't exactly indicative of the average American woman," Annie said.

Adam turned a smile her way. "Movies never are," he said. "They're like dreams. You know sometimes that's how I feel about my memories of Candace. They're like dreams as well."

"Do you know why she left?" Annie asked gently.

"A misunderstanding," he said. "I'm not really good at talking about my feelings. Or talking at all, I suppose. I just took Candace for granted. She was such a quiet, steady ray of sunshine, and I thought she would always be there. Or at least until I was willing to tell her how I felt ... until I was willing to share my secrets with her."

"It sounds like she was very important to you," Annie said.

He nodded. "Maybe I'm just fooling myself with this search. Sometimes when one misses a moment, there's no catching up with it again. I suppose I should go back to England and focus on my work like a sensible person."

Annie felt the secret of the little cats pressing on her. If she told him about the mysterious gifts, he would certainly not leave until he tracked down the answer. Finally, she looked straight into his troubled face. "I think you should stay a little longer," she said. "I think it's too soon to give up."

His countenance lightened. "You really think so?"

"I do."

He smiled slightly. "You're a bit of sunshine your own self, aren't you?"

"I don't know about that," Annie said, laughing. "But I guess I like every story to have a happy ending."

"Wouldn't that be lovely?" he asked.

Tartan had been sitting in the sand looking patiently back and forth between Annie and Adam as they talked, but clearly the schnauzer had used up his daily supply of patience, because he suddenly jumped up and began tugging hard at the leash.

"Apparently I need to get back to my walk," Annie said.

Adam laughed. "And I will get back to my search. Thanks for cheering me."

"You're welcome," she said as Tartan tugged her down the beach. As Annie followed Tartan, she thought about what Adam had told her and marveled at how it echoed some of the conversation she'd had with Alice in the parking lot of the church. Was she acting like Adam, simply assuming that Ian would always be around?

Annie chased her thoughts in circles as she walked. Suddenly she realized she'd gone quite some distance from the parking lot, and she tugged Tartan in a circle to head back. The sun was nearly directly overhead, and Annie felt a grumble in her stomach. "I'll get you home," she told the dog. "And then I think I'd better get some lunch before I head over to the vet's office."

Tartan wagged his tail at the sound of her voice. Annie noticed he wasn't nearly as bouncy and wondered if she could possibly have finally worn out Ian's dog. *That would be a first*, she thought.

Tartan seemed glad to finally reach the car, and he curled up in the backseat with a sigh. Still, by the time she got to Ian's, the dog had rallied and demanded considerable petting before Annie left him with fresh water and food. As she bent to pet him, her stomach grumbled so loudly that Tartan looked at her in surprise.

"Time for lunch," she told him with a last chin rub. "I'll be back this evening for another walk."

Once on the road again, she briefly considered driving to The Cup & Saucer and grabbing some lunch there, but her shoes felt a little damp and gritty from the walk on the beach, and she really wanted to change them. So she drove home to a chorus of grumbles from her stomach.

"Goodness," she said as she stopped to grab her mail from the box. "You'd think I hadn't eaten in a week." She began leafing through the mail as she headed up the porch steps and caught sight of something out of the corner of her eye. A small package lay in one of the wicker chairs.

Since she wasn't expecting a delivery, she retrieved the box with some excitement, only to see that it wasn't sent by any delivery company. The box was completely blank with no address labels. Someone had left it on the porch.

Annie sat down in the wicker chair and carefully slit the paper tape that held the box closed with her fingernail. She opened the box and gasped. In a cloud of tissue paper, a chubby gray cat stood up on its hind legs, batting two white paws in the air. The needle-felted cat looked so much like Boots it was uncanny.

Annie gently poked through the tissue, looking for a card. She found it tucked in close to one side of the box. The careful lettering matched all the other cat sculptures. The card read, "Because of Betsy, I survived. I thank her in my heart every day."

Annie touched the tiny cat's soft wool fur and shook her head in amazement. "Where are you, Candace Caine?" she whispered. Somehow this mysterious woman was eating at the diner, worshipping at the church, using the library, and shopping at A Stitch in Time, and no one had any idea who she was. Now she'd been right on Annie's porch. Had Annie passed her in town hundreds of times without knowing it was her? Could one of the people she saw regularly really be Candace Caine incognito?

~ 17 ~

After a light brunch, Annie changed her clothes and washed her hands several times before giving Boots some attention. The cat sniffed Annie's hand suspiciously and then rubbed against her and purred when she didn't detect the dreaded dog scent.

"I know it's been hard on you," Annie said, "having to share me with Tartan. He's really a very nice dog."

The fact that Boots continued to purr and rub her face against Annie's fingers certainly proved the cat did not speak English. Annie sat on the sofa for a few minutes, lavishing attention on Boots. She glanced toward her project bag with a small pang of guilt. She only needed to sew the parts of the cap together and she'd have the twins' Easter gifts done. If she did it now, she could mail the hats while she was in town.

As eager as Annie was to chase the mystery, she forced herself to focus on the monkey cap so her stitching would be neat and even. When she finished, she walked back through the house to the small library where she knew she'd left a box. She wrapped the caps in tissue paper, added a note for the twins, and then slipped all of it into the box and sealed it. She carried the package to the living room, collected the little box with the miniature Boots inside, and headed out the door.

Tucking the little box into the glove compartment of the

Malibu, Annie stood and looked across the yard into Alice's driveway. The Mustang wasn't there, so Annie would have to make this drive alone. She didn't want to put off the trip to the Stony Point Veterinary Clinic to ask about the Friends of St. Francis.

Annie drove up to the small Georgian home that housed the clinic on the first floor and Janet Martin's living quarters on the second floor. The house had the clean, strictly symmetrical façade that was typical of the really old Georgian houses all over New England. Heavy modillion moldings underneath the roofline eave were balanced by thick window heads above the first story windows.

A small neat sign next to the front door was the only clue that the historical house was more than just a private home. Though she'd been to the clinic a number of times for Boots's checkups, Annie marveled once again at how often business locations in New England were marked with tiny signs. It was nothing like the huge signs, often standing well above building height, that she saw so often back in Texas.

Annie opened the door and the sense of a private home ended as the door opened into a foyer with clear signs pointing visitors toward the admissions area. In the large, bright admissions room, a row of chairs faced a long desk where an older teenager talked on the phone. Annie recognized her from past visits. The girl wore her straight hair in a neat bob; several streaks of sky blue contrasted sharply with the coal black of the rest of the girl's hair.

Most of the chairs in the waiting room were full. Annie recognized several of the people from church, and they smiled and nodded at her. The girl at the desk looked up with concern as she hung up the phone. "Mrs. Dawson," she said. "I hope Boots isn't sick."

"No, the only thing Boots is suffering from is annoyance," Annie said.

The girl looked at her quizzically.

"I'm watching Tartan while the mayor is away," Annie said. "Boots is not one of Tartan's bigger fans."

The girl's eyes opened wide. "You have them both in the same house?"

"No," Annie laughed. "I don't know if Grey Gables would survive that. I'm going over to Ian's house a couple times a day, but since I come home smelling of Tartan, Boots is giving me the cold shoulder."

The girl giggled. "So do you need an appointment?"

"Actually, I was hoping to chat with Dr. Martin about something," Annie said. "It'll only take a few minutes, but it looks like she's very busy."

"A little, but most of these folks are going to be quick in-and-outs. If you don't mind waiting, I can go see if Dr. Martin thinks she'll be able to squeeze in a quick chat."

"Thanks."

Annie walked over and sat by Chessey Cushman, who held a small pet carrier in her lap. Annie peeked into the carrier and spotted a tiny, mostly bald poodle shivering inside. "Is your dog sick?" she asked.

Chessey shook her head. "No, Don Juan shivers like that all the time. Dr. Martin said it's quite common in dogs of his age. He actually feels fine; he just needs an s-h-o-t."

Annie smiled a little, wondering if Chessey really thought her dog could spell. "Chessey, do you happen to remember the Friends of St. Francis? I think it was some kind of animal shelter."

"Oh yes, I remember it. I even volunteered there some when I was younger," she said. "They were lovely people. Don Juan didn't come from there, of course. He's purebred."

"I think Boots may have come from the Friends of St. Francis," Annie said. "She was Gram's cat, and I inherited her with Grey Gables."

"It's possible," Chessey said. "I wouldn't know. I wasn't really involved with the adoption side. I mostly cleaned pens for the few animals they kept there at the main house. Most of the animals were fostered in homes all over Stony Point."

Annie didn't know what else to ask, so she sat back quietly. In a few minutes, she heard someone open the front door, followed by several loud thumps and disgruntled yowls. Finally, Nancy Breaker appeared in the doorway, struggling to carry a huge pet carrier. She managed to slam the carrier against the door frame and then again against the reception desk. Each thump produced more yowling from inside the carrier.

An older man who sat next to an elderly Labrador retriever stood up quickly and took a few steps toward the desk. "May I help you?" he asked.

"No, no—I'm fine," Nancy said, turning to smile at him and smacking the carrier against the desk again, producing more yowls.

"Dr. Martin will be with you shortly," the receptionist said, looking with alarm at the large pet carrier. "You can have a seat."

Nancy looked around the room and caught sight of Annie. She broke into a big smile and staggered across the room with the carrier. She practically fell into the seat beside Annie, dropping the carrier on the floor between her feet. "I'm so glad to see you, Mrs. Dawson," she said. "Have you thought about the parade of homes tour?"

"I'm really thinking I might prefer not to participate," Annie said.

"But Grey Gables is so lovely," she said. "You can be proud of what you've done for the place. Here, wait, look at how beautiful your home would look to people on the tour." She rooted in the large handbag she had slung over her shoulder and pulled out a glossy paper with "Parade of Homes" printed across the top. On the sheet Annie spotted photos of several Stony Point homes, including both Stella Brickson's house and Grey Gables!

"I can't believe you're using Grey Gables on advertising when I haven't given permission," Annie said testily. "And I'm certain Stella wouldn't be pleased to see this either."

Nancy blinked at her in surprise, her large glasses making her look doubly shocked. "I'm not using your house on advertising. I printed this just for some of the more reluctant homeowners—to show you how nice your home would look on the tour!"

"Well, be certain *not* to put Grey Gables on the actual advertising," Annie said. "I don't want to be on the tour."

"But your house is so lovely," Nancy said. "Really, you should be proud of what you've done."

"I am," Annie said, "but I know I would obsess over every detail if I let the house be part of the tour. I tend to be a worrier. I'd make myself sick over it. I'm absolutely decided about it."

The other woman sighed. "I really thought we'd get more response than we have. There are so many lovely homes here. I wonder if it's me. I know I can be too gobby and a lot of people don't like that."

"Gobby?" Annie echoed.

Nancy chuckled. "Sorry about that. It means talkative. Some people in the States might say 'gabby.' I lived in Britain for several years when I was younger. You pick up the oddest slang when you live in a place. You should hear my nieces laugh at me when I call their athletic shoes 'trainers.'"

Annie looked at the woman a moment, stunned. Nancy was certainly a little woman and about Annie's age. And she was plump. She remembered Adam saying that Candace Caine was not as thin as American women in the movies. Could this be the woman Adam was searching for?

"Is something wrong?" Nancy asked.

"Oh, no, I'm fine," Annie said, still feeling stunned. "I just thought of something. Did you enjoy living in Britain?"

"For the most part," she said as she sat back in her seat. "I can't imagine living anywhere but Stony Point now. I've always felt at home here."

"Yes," Annie said. "I feel that way too."

"Of course, now I'm having such a horrible time getting enough homes for the tour." She patted Annie's hand. "Which does not mean I'm still trying to talk you into it. I heard you loud and clear."

"Have you talked to Gwendolyn Palmer?" Annie asked hesitantly. "She mentioned that she wouldn't mind having Wedgwood on the tour."

Nancy's eyes grew wide behind her round lenses.

"Really? That would be brilliant. They have such lovely roses. I've never been terribly successful with roses, though I've planted them all around my cottage. I suspect they don't get enough sun with the willow trees."

"Is that why you want roses on the Town Square?" Annie asked. "I'm afraid I agree with Mary Beth about how impractical that would be. So many children play there when the tourists come in the summer."

"I suppose," Nancy said. "I've never had children, and I don't think about them all that much. My cats are as close as I come to kiddies." She leaned down to coo into the front of the pet carrier. A paw darted out and batted at the laces on Nancy's very sensible shoes. Nancy patted the paw, and it darted back into the carrier.

"Mrs. Dawson?"

Annie looked up to find the teenager from the front desk standing in the doorway. She gestured to Annie. Even though she wanted more time to talk with Nancy, Annie hurried over. "I talked to Dr. Martin, and she's leaving as soon as these appointments are finished. She is making a house call on one of our elderly clients. Her shih tzu isn't well, and the owner doesn't drive. The doctor said to tell you that she'd call you at home this evening if that's OK."

"That would be great," Annie said. "Thanks." She glanced back at Nancy who was talking into the cat carrier. Nancy had lived in Britain and loved cats. She also clearly cared about Stony Point, and Kate had said she was very good with fine crochet thread. Still, she didn't sound overly fond of children for a picture-book author. Plus, it was simply difficult to imagine someone pining away for the woman, though Annie immediately felt bad about having that thought.

"Is there something else?" the receptionist asked.

"No, I was just woolgathering," Annie said. "Thank you again. Please tell Dr. Martin that I'll look forward to her call. And assure her it's not related to Boots, or not to her health anyway. I know Janet tends to worry about her patients.

"She does do that," the teenager agreed.

Annie thanked her again and headed toward the door. Suddenly she was struck by an idea. Maybe there was a clue to the mystery that she'd overlooked.

— 18 —

nnie turned abruptly and headed back toward Nancy. "Could you tell me how many times you photographed Grey Gables?" she asked. "I think I saw you twice."

"Well, it wasn't actually me taking the photos," Nancy said. "I paid my neighbor's daughter because she's good with a camera. I'm sorry it made you angry."

"That's OK," Annie said. "So was it more than twice?"

"Yes," Nancy admitted. "I went back and took another photo this morning because I noticed you'd put out all those lovely pansies, and I felt they added a nice touch of color. I won't use that photo, of course."

"This morning?" Annie asked. "Did you happen to notice anyone on my porch?"

Nancy smiled and shook her head. "I was hurrying so you wouldn't catch me. Would you believe Stella Brickson actually sent Jason out to yell at me when I took the photos of her house? I didn't want that to happen again."

Annie could completely picture Stella sending Jason after Nancy, and she fought the urge to smile. "Do you suppose I could see the photo you took today?"

"Of course," Nancy replied. "I have the camera with me." She rummaged in her bag again and soon pulled out a small digital camera. She turned the camera on and flipped through the photos on the small view screen. When she reached the photo of Grey Gables, the small screen made it virtually impossible to tell if someone was on the porch.

"Oh, I wish I could see it bigger," Annie said.

"I can email you a copy," Nancy said. She rummaged again for a notebook and took Annie's email address. "I'll send it as soon as I get home. It won't be as good as the other photo you saw. I'm not the best photographer."

"I'd appreciate seeing it just the same," Annie said. She thanked Nancy and headed out of the clinic.

She was soon driving toward Main Street to mail the package to LeeAnn and then talk with Mary Beth and Kate. When she passed the Stony Point Community Church, Annie suddenly had an idea and turned into the lot. If Nancy was the cat sculptor, she would need to be an active part of the church to have access to the storage room.

As she slipped into the back door, she heard music and followed the sound to the big meeting room where a large group of women were hopping and lunging and swinging their arms in time to the music. The exercise class was one of the many groups that used a portion of the church during the week. Annie sighed, remembering the long list that the church secretary had ticked off. The number of people who might be familiar with the storage room could indeed include everyone in Stony Point!

Still, as long as she was there, she decided to chat with Ellen Whitaker again. Adam was so certain that Candace would be involved with children in some capacity, so Annie wanted to ask Ellen if Nancy was a Sunday school volunteer.

She found the cheerful young woman standing out in the hall in front of the office, humming to herself. Ellen turned away from the bulletin board where she was pinning things and smiled. "Mrs. Dawson, how are you?"

"Great," Annie said as she stepped up to admire Ellen's work. The bulletin board was covered in a lovely spring floral pattern. Across the top, it read, "Volunteers Spring Up All Over." All over the board, various photos were pinned up. "It looks like the church has a lot of volunteers."

Ellen nodded. "We're very blessed. Every time Reverend Wallace asks for help, people step right up. Though some people take on so much that I worry about them."

Annie pointed to one photo that showed a group of smiling women. "Who are they?"

"They teach children's Sunday school," Ellen said. "They're one of the groups I worry about, some of them take on nursery duties during the main service as well as Sunday school before. They just love the kids so much."

Interested, Annie looked closer. She didn't see Nancy. "Is this everyone who works with the children?"

"All the regulars," Ellen said. "Sometimes teens will help out in the baby nursery, and I didn't manage to get Peggy Carson in the photo."

"Oh?" Annie said. "I didn't know Peggy taught Sunday school."

"She doesn't do it all the time," Ellen said. "She's our backup, though she's had to fill in a lot more than usual this year with Ivy being sick so much. But Peggy is great with the kids, and Emily is always so excited every time her mom is the classroom leader."

"Do you have any other backups?" Annie asked. "Anyone named Nancy?"

Ellen shook her head, smiling. "Do you want to be added to the roster? I think we're OK in the classrooms, but we can always use someone else in the nursery rotation. We hate to have the same people missing the service all the time. The teens are great, but we like having an adult in there with them in case of emergencies. And to be honest, diapers are changed more often if we have an adult in there."

"That sounds like fun," Annie said. "It's been a long time since I've spent an hour or so holding babies."

Ellen beamed and promised to put her on the list. "Someone will call you to talk about the schedule."

Annie headed out of the church feeling a little disappointed. She didn't think that she'd learned anything valuable, but she was glad she'd be helping out in the nursery. With the twins in school already and no new grandchildren in the plans, Annie did sometimes miss the special feeling of holding a baby.

She stopped in at the post office and was greeted by Norma, the only employee she ever saw there. Annie noticed that Norma's perm had grown out some and the longer, softer curls gave the rather plain woman a feminine softness to her face. Norma actually smiled as Annie placed her package on the counter. "Sending something to the twins?" Norma asked.

Annie looked at her in surprise. Norma was normally even less chatty than Stella and definitely did not believe in small talk. "Yes," Annie said. "Easter gifts."

"That's great; I'm sure they'll enjoy them."

As Norma weighed the package, Annie decided to risk a

question. "Do you know if someone named Candace Caine lives in Stony Point?"

Norma's face darkened slightly. "It's like I told that British fella, I can't give out information on Stony Point residents."

"Oh, I understand," Annie said, realizing that Adam had beat her there.

"Now, since you *are* a Stony Point resident," Norma said. "I'd be willing to tell *you* that we certainly haven't delivered any mail to anyone by that name."

"Oh—thanks."

As Norma took Annie's money for the postage, she looked at the cash register where she spotted a small orange-striped cat sitting in a miniature letter carrier's bag. "Oh, you got a cat too!"

"The post office did," Norma agreed with a warm smile. "Someone really appreciates our service to the community."

"I can see that," Annie said. "That cat is lovely. Would you mind if I snapped a picture of it? I'm collecting photos of all the cats around town."

"That would be fine," Norma said. "We're very proud of it. You know, you can think no one notices the work you do in a job like this, but when I look at that little cat, I know someone noticed. Can you imagine the hours someone put in just for us?" She smiled fondly at the little sculpture.

"I'm sure it's well deserved," Annie told her as she snapped the photos. "Did you get a card with it?"

"Yes, and it's so cute, look!" Norma thrust the card toward Annie.

Annie took it and snapped a photo from her phone. She immediately recognized the handwriting as she read it:

"Neither snow, nor rain, nor gloom of night can keep me from saying thank you."

After the post office, the drive to A Stitch in Time was quick. Annie grabbed her cat sculpture from the glove compartment and slipped it into her project bag before hopping out of the car. The shop was bustling, so Annie settled into one of the comfy chairs and pulled out some scrap yarn to whip up a quick bazaar toy until the shop crowd thinned down. Now and then, Mary Beth cast her a curious glance, but Annie just smiled.

In spite of herself, Annie was soon caught up in the crochet. The little toy was simple, but it still required Annie's attention since the rows were short and changed lengths often. Annie was so caught up in the counting that she jumped when Kate put a hand on her shoulder.

"Sorry, I didn't mean to startle you," Kate said as she slipped into the chair beside Annie. "I love these little toys you've made for the bazaar. I need to do more quick crochet items. Did you come into the shop for help with these? It doesn't really look like you need any."

"No, these are easy," Annie said. Then she added, almost in a whisper, "I came to talk about the mystery."

Kate's eyes widened. "Really. Have you learned anything new?"

Annie nodded. "Two new cats and maybe a theory. I was waiting until the shop was empty."

"It's coming up on lunchtime," Kate said. "We tend to get a lull while everyone is eating lunch."

Annie looked around. The bustle had thinned down to two women rummaging around the pattern racks.

Finally the women settled on a pattern and carried it to the counter. Annie folded her crochet hook into the toy she was working on, rolling her scrap-craft pattern book around the whole thing and slipping the rubber band that she'd had on her wrist over it. Annie had found that keeping an active project rolled up in the pattern book at least slowed Boots down when she managed to find the project bag unattended.

The two customers chatted happily with Mary Beth at the counter. Mary Beth managed to avoid sounding impatient, but her eyes darted toward Annie several times. When the women finally left, Mary Beth practically launched herself from behind the counter. "What's up?" she asked as she crossed the room.

Annie blinked at her innocently. "I was just working on a bazaar project—unless it's too late to add anything."

Mary Beth stopped and put her hands on her hips. "It *is* pretty late. If you finish more toys, just bring them to the bazaar, and we can tag them at the table. But I know you're not really here for that—something's up. Kate looks as excited as I feel."

Annie relented and fished the little box out of her bag. "Look what I found on my porch today."

Mary Beth opened the box and both women cooed over the miniature version of Boots. "It looks like the artist definitely knows about Boots."

"That's too much resemblance to be a coincidence," Kate agreed. "So it must be someone you know."

Annie shook her head. "Not necessarily. Look at the card. It's someone Gram knew."

"And Betsy Holden knew every soul in Stony Point," Mary Beth said with a groan.

"There's more," Annie said. "I'm certain that the person who wrote that card is Candace Caine."

Now Mary Beth and Kate both gaped at her. "What makes you think that?" Mary Beth asked.

"The library assistant in the children's section showed me one of Candace Caine's picture books, and the handwriting on the card matches the writing in the illustrations," Annie said. "Plus, Gram had two Candace Caine books in the attic. Alice and I checked—they match these cards too. One of the books had an inscription and that writing matched too. Candace Caine is definitely the one giving these little cats."

"How does this mystery woman manage to be everywhere in Stony Point?" Mary Beth said. "It's like having a ghost. She comes and goes, and no one knows who she is."

"I wondered if it might be Nancy from the Garden Club." Annie said.

Mary Beth laughed. "No. Really? Why?"

"Well, Adam Smithfield said Candace Caine was an American, but she lived several years in England," Annie said, "and Nancy told me today that she'd spent several years in London. Plus, you told me that she could do the tiny crocheted lace on your cat's pillow. And she clearly loves cats. She had a pet carrier at the vet's today with more than one cat in it."

"She definitely has cats," Kate said. "I had to sit beside her at a church luncheon once, and my allergies acted up so badly I could barely breathe. I asked her if she had a cat, and she said she had four!"

"Well, sure, she has cats and can make lace," Mary Beth said. "But there's a huge difference between being able to make lace and being able to make these little cats. I just can't see Nancy doing that."

"Adam also described Candace as a little woman," Annie said, "but not as skinny as American movies showed. That tends to fit Nancy."

Mary Beth crossed her arms. "That also describes *me*."

"Do any other customers jump to mind with that description?" Annie asked.

"A few. I could make a list," Mary Beth said. "Kate can help."

"We'll have to keep in mind that weight can change," Kate said. "You know, when you combine shortness and the ability to do that fine crochet, Nancy does fit."

"She may fit the *clues*," Mary Beth said, shaking her head, "but I can't picture anyone following Nancy to the ends of the earth."

"It's hard to say what love will do," Kate said.

Annie sighed. "There is one other area where Nancy doesn't fit. Adam was certain that wherever Candace is, she must be working with children. And Nancy doesn't seem to work with children. From my chat with her, she didn't seem to like them very much."

"I suppose she could be pretending not to like kids," Kate said, doubt clear in her voice.

"I don't think Nancy is that subtle," Mary Beth said. "Or subtle at all."

"Well then," Annie said sadly, "that leaves me with a sad lack of suspects."

"Wait a second," Kate said. "You told me there were two new cats. Yours is one, who got the other?"

"Norma showed me one at the post office," Annie said. "You'll have to go by and see it. She's so proud of it that she's actually pleasant. The little cat is sitting in the tiniest letter carrier's bag. The attention to detail in all of these sculptures is amazing."

"Well, since everyone in Stony Point goes to the post office at one point or another, that doesn't exactly help us narrow down our suspects. The list is still basically every woman in Stony Point."

"Well, I'm certain it's Candace Caine, and that she's not using her real name here. Norma told me that no one in Stony Point named Candace Caine gets mail."

"We keep piling up clues without really getting much closer to the answer," Mary Beth said.

"That's exactly how I feel," Annie admitted. "I'm beginning to think this may be the mystery we never solve."

～ 19 ～

"You know," Mary Beth said as her eyes turned back to the tiny cat in her hands. "There's something very familiar about this writing."

"Isn't it the same writing that was on the card with your cat?" Annie asked.

"Yes," Mary Beth said, her eyes still on the card, "but it's more than that. It's the capital I. I didn't have a capital I on my card. I've seen this before. It's really quite unique compared to the other letters. See? It's much more ornate."

Annie stood and looked at the card. The writer had put more of a flourish on her capital I. "Maybe Candace Caine wrote you a note sometime. She might have started with I."

"Maybe," Mary Beth said dubiously, "but I still think I saw this recently, and I don't get a lot of notes from customers. Let me think about it for a while. It'll come to me. So, you said you saw Nancy with a pet carrier; were you at Dr. Martin's?"

"I was at the clinic, but I didn't get to see the doctor because she was so busy. She's supposed to call me this evening," Annie said. "This mystery seems to leave me *almost* making connections all over."

"Well, I thought of another near connection," Mary Beth said. "I asked one of my older customers about the Friends of St. Francis this morning. She remembered them, though she never went there. But a friend of hers volunteered for them."

"Oh! Maybe I could talk to the friend," Annie said.

"I'm thinking you could," Mary Beth said with a smile. "It's Josephine Booth."

Annie blinked in surprise. "Well, that's great. Someone I *know* I can go talk to. Thanks, Mary Beth." She looked down at her watch. "I should be able to catch her, so I'm going right over to the library."

As Annie hurried down the sidewalk toward the library, she shivered. The pleasant morning was settling into a chilly afternoon. She glanced up at the sky and spotted gray clouds on the horizon. "I'll have to be sure to get Tartan's second walk in soon," she murmured.

At the library, she quickly found Josephine sorting through a pile of books. She turned a warm smile on Annie. "You look like a woman on a mission," Josephine said.

"I actually wanted to ask you about the Friends of St. Francis," Annie said. "You volunteered there, right?"

Josephine nodded. "That was a while ago, of course. I never felt like I really had the time to devote to a pet of my own, but I was able to help out by offering a temporary home to a cat now and then."

"Do you happen to know anything about how Gram got Boots?" Annie asked. "I understand Boots came from the Friends of St. Francis."

"That's right, she did," Josephine said. "I remember how happy your grandmother was about it."

"So Gram came in and picked out the kitten?" Annie asked.

Josephine paused, her face clouded as she chased the memory. "Yes, she came in with a friend of hers to look over the kittens. I think the actual adoption happened on a different day though. Maybe your grandmother needed some time to think about which one she wanted."

"Do you know the name of the woman who was with Gram?" Annie asked.

"After all these years?" Josephine asked incredulously. "I'm not even sure I heard it, though I've seen her around town, of course. She comes to the library now and then."

Annie felt a surge of excitement. "Do you know what she looks like now?"

"Not so different really," Josephine said. "Thinner, and shorter than me by quite a bit. She isn't at all chatty."

That certainly leaves out Nancy, Annie thought.

"A lot of our patrons come to the library for a quiet time of reading," Josephine continued. "We try to accommodate what each person wants. We'll chat with the chatty ones and leave the quiet ones in peace if they seem to want that."

"And she seems to want that," Annie said.

"I'm not sure," Josephine admitted. "She's very polite, but somehow she seems sad."

Annie was struck by how much that reminded her of Adam. Was Candace Caine pining for him as much as he was for her? "Does she help out with the children's library?"

Josephine looked surprised. "Oh, no, I can't imagine. She seems like the sort who would be scared to death of the kids. Our little ones can be a little boisterous."

Annie felt a pang of worry. That didn't exactly match Adam's assurance that Candace would definitely be involved with children. "Do you know of anyone here who might know the woman's name?"

"I don't know—maybe. You could ask."

"It might help if you could be more specific about what she looks like," said Annie.

"Well, there's something about her that makes you not want to look at her too long."

"Like a deformity?" Annie asked.

"Oh no, nothing like that. It's more like it would be painful to her if you noticed her too much. At any rate, she's a shorter woman, as I said, with brown hair. About your age, I imagine."

Annie went to each of the people working in the library and asked about Candace, as described by Josephine. Although each person said the library had some very shy patrons, and even mentioned a few names, they were always different names. Annie had never imagined that Stony Point had so many shy women.

"Every town has shy women," Grace Emory said when Annie voiced her thought aloud in the reference section. "Women who've experienced too much pain, too much unpleasantness in life. They just want to be left alone, and I think we respond to that instinctively. We don't notice them, and the library offers a nice refuge. You can see people, but everyone is occupied with their own reasons for being here. So you can be left alone, if you want."

Annie thanked Grace and headed out of the library. As she walked across the Town Square and down the street to where she had parked her car, in front of A Stitch in Time, Annie thought about the other places that had gotten the tiny cats from Candace Caine. Did they offer her the same thing as the library? Did they give her a safe place to be out in the world but not touched by it? Certainly in the bustle of the diner, you could be surrounded by movement but have your own bubble. Annie had often felt that way when she'd stopped there for a cup of tea and a chance to process whatever was going on in her life at the time.

Annie had reached her car and glanced toward the door of the diner as she thought about it. She wouldn't mind stopping for a cup of tea, but then she heard a rumble of thunder in the distance. She needed to drive over and walk Tartan before the rain moved in.

At Ian's house, Annie found Tartan back to his normal, excited self. "I can't promise to wear you out again," Annie said as she snapped on his leash, "but we'd better take a trot around the neighborhood before the rain starts."

Tartan trotted obediently at Annie's side as she walked. She glanced nervously at the darkening sky, hoping they could finish the walk before the rain started. She picked up her pace, and Tartan cheerfully matched it.

"Annie! Annie Dawson!"

Annie stopped and turned to see Nancy hurrying down a driveway just a few doors away from Ian's house. Annie glanced curiously up at what must be Nancy's house. Early spring had not yet awakened the cottage-style home's garden. Annie could tell that the plantings had been carefully chosen to create an almost Thomas Kincaid, English cottage effect—an effect that would reach its colorful zenith in the early summer.

"Your yard is lovely," Annie said as Nancy caught up

to her, puffing. Annie noticed that Nancy kept a careful distance from Tartan and his slightly muddy paws.

Nancy beamed. "Thank you! I do work at it. Do you know when Ian will be home?"

Annie smiled and shook her head. "No, I still don't know."

"Do you suppose you could leave him this note?" Nancy offered a fancy envelope with Ian's name on it in ornate script. Looking at it, Annie knew that Nancy's handwriting looked nothing like Candace Caine's.

"I'll be glad to," Annie said. "I'll put it right on his desk when I get home with Tartan. Did you happen to email that photo?"

"Oh no, I forgot," Nancy said. "I'll do it right away."

"Thank you. We best get back to our walk since I believe it's going to rain."

Nancy looked at the sky in alarm and scurried back into her house. Annie slipped the envelope into her cardigan pocket. "Now this note I'll be sure to remember," Annie said to Tartan; he yipped in agreement.

Thunder rumbled in the distance, and Annie trotted along the sidewalk with the schnauzer. Tartan seemed delighted by the fast pace and was still ready for more running when Annie had to stop to gasp for a minute. He hopped up, putting his paws on Annie's leg and wagged his tail furiously.

"You could pretend to be tired," she said.

Tartan just barked and licked her hand. They continued at a slightly slower pace with Annie casting nervous glances at the sky. Finally, they finished the lap around the neighborhood and started up Ian's long driveway. That's when the sky seemed to open up and rain pounded down on Annie and Tartan.

Tartan clearly didn't mind the rain either, though he snapped at the falling drops now and then. They trudged up the long driveway, and Annie tugged Tartan gently toward the side of the house. They'd go in the back door since Annie certainly didn't want to leave puddles all through Ian's house. Suddenly Annie froze at the sound of a car on the driveway. The rain had drowned out the sound of the approaching car until it was very close.

Annie turned around sharply and saw Ian's sleek car roll to a stop. With a sinking feeling, she pushed a hank of dripping hair away from her face.

"Oh Annie!" Ian called, rushing through the rain to her side. Tartan went wild at the end of the leash, lunging for Ian and barking with joy. Ian took the leash gently from Annie's icy hand. "Let's get you inside."

He began leading her toward the front door as Tartan splashed in all the puddles along the way. "No, Ian," Annie said. "We should go in the back. We'll drip all over your floors."

"They're just floors," Ian said. "We need to get you in out of the cold."

Annie gave in and let him lead her into the house. Annie could feel the water running off her in streams. "Hold Tartan here," Ian said. "I'll get towels."

He disappeared down the hall but came back quickly with thick towels. Annie accepted hers gratefully and rubbed most of the water out of her hair so it would stop dripping freezing streams down her back. Ian briskly toweled Tartan dry.

"We need to get you into some dry clothes," Ian said as he stood and looked Annie over. She was certain she must look exactly like a half-drowned rat.

"It's OK," she said. "I'll just run to the car and head home. I can change there."

Ian reached out and put his warm hand on her arm. "Your skin is ice cold. You can't go back out in the rain until you warm up. Especially since you were only caught out in the rain because you were doing a favor for me. Here, take off your shoes, and we'll make a run for the bathroom."

Annie slipped off her shoes and dashed for the bathroom with Ian. In her bare feet, the drips of water from her still soggy clothes made her slip and slide as she hurried. Several times Ian had to catch her to keep her on her feet. Finally, they reached the tiled bathroom floor.

"OK, you get out of those wet things and take a hot shower," he said. "I'll find you something dry to put on. It won't be stylish, but I should be able to manage something warm. Then we'll fill you with warm tea, and we can wait together until the rain stops."

"Oh Ian," Annie said. "Not much of a homecoming, is it?"

"I can't think of anything I'd like better than rescuing you from the rain," Ian said with a smile. "Now, out of those wet clothes."

He closed the door, and Annie quickly took off her sky blue linen pants, which had grown so wet they stuck to her legs like skin. And then she removed her cute sleeveless cotton sweater and matching cardigan, which had sagged from the water until the neckline of the sleeveless sweater was almost indecent and the sleeves of the cardigan nearly covered her hands.

Annie looked sadly at the pants, hoping they weren't ruined. She piled her clothes loosely in the sink and stepped into the shower. She hadn't realized how frozen she was until the hot water seemed to pound heat through her skin. It was wonderful.

At one point, Annie heard a soft rap at the bathroom door. Ian called out that he was slipping a change of clothes on the counter inside the door. When Annie finally felt like her body temperature must be close to human again, she shut off the water and pulled open the shower door. Annie dried off quickly and picked up the clothes. The T-shirt was a faded blue gray with a whale screen-printed on the front. She recognized it as one she'd seen Ian wear to a summer picnic on the Town Square. She slipped it over her head, and it engulfed her.

The sweatpants folded under the shirt were much smaller and clearly had belonged to a woman. They were a little long but otherwise fit well. Annie thought they must have belonged to Ian's wife, Arianna, and felt a little strange about wearing them. She slipped her feet into a too-large pair of warm socks and then ran her fingers through her hair to try to get it into some sort of order.

Finally, she tiptoed out of the bathroom and went looking for Ian. She found him in the kitchen, pouring hot water into tall mugs. "Perfect timing," he said, "as usual."

Annie laughed. "If I'd had perfect timing, I wouldn't have been half-drowned by the rain."

"But then, I wouldn't have been greeted by my favorite dog sitter," Ian said. "I hope Tartan didn't give you any trouble."

"No, of course not. I'm beginning to understand dog people," Annie said. "Tartan is wonderful company."

"He certainly makes it difficult to be gloomy," Ian said as he handed Annie a mug and led her toward a chair. He sat near her and gently lifted a strand of hair away from her face.

"How was your trip?" Annie asked tentatively.

Ian sighed. "Sad and stressful. But my mother-in-law passed in her sleep. I think the whole family was in shock, even though she'd been so sick and so unhappy. You never know whether it's OK to be a little relieved along with your sadness."

"It sounds like a difficult few days," Annie agreed.

"Being back with Arianna's family was strange," Ian said. "I was glad to see them, but I guess it made me realize how much I still miss her too."

Annie nodded. "I know that feeling. I love Wayne's relatives, and I try to see them when I'm in Texas, but it's hard too."

Ian reached out and put a hand over hers. "It's nice to have someone who knows exactly how that feels." He shook his head. "After Arianna died, it was like she'd been erased from history by some people. They never mentioned her, never brought up old memories."

Annie nodded. "I suppose they didn't know what to say."

"I know," he said. "And sometimes when people did say something, they said things that didn't really help. They meant well, but it was just too much. That's why I had to get away from Stony Point for a while right after Arianna died. In New York, all of the bustle and noise was a nice distraction."

"I guess that was part of what made coming to Stony Point so appealing," Annie agreed. "I had good memories here, but also, the town was full of people who saw me as Annie, not as Wayne's widow."

Ian nodded with understanding. For a few minutes after that, they each sipped their tea in silence, lost in thoughts of the past. It wasn't an awkward silence though. It felt friendly and comforting to Annie.

Finally Ian looked over at her and smiled. "Thanks again for taking care of Tartan. And I spotted my mail on my desk, so thanks for picking that up as well."

"Oh!" Annie said, hopping out of her chair. "I have one more note for you."

She padded down the hall to the bathroom and pulled Nancy's note from the pocket of her long cotton sweater. The envelope was soaked and floppy, and the handwriting on the outside was unreadable. She carried it back to the kitchen. "I'm afraid the rain seems to have ruined it."

Ian took it from her. "What was it?"

"A note from Nancy Breaker, from across the street," she said. "I expect she wants to put your house on the Garden Club's parade of homes. I figure that's what it's about."

"What does that entail?" he asked.

"I really don't know," she said. "I turned her down for

Grey Gables, so I haven't gotten all the details, but she can be very insistent. She even took photos of my house and made a mock-up of the brochure. So, good luck if you decide to say no."

Ian lifted the envelope flap and gently slid out a water-logged sheet of computer paper that tore when he tried to unfold it. Finally he laid it out on the table, and they peered at it. The general layout of the smears made Annie suspect it had looked much like the paper Nancy had shown her, but it had soaked together into a blurry mess of color-printer ink. "I guess I'll have to call her," he said with a shrug. Then he looked up at Annie and smiled. "So, tell me what you've been up to besides walking my dog. Any mysteries?"

Annie knew he was teasing her, and she was rewarded by a surprised look when she nodded. "Actually, yes. We have a missing lost love, a mysterious artist, and a tall, dark stranger in town."

"Any kidnappings, break-ins, or threats of violence?" Ian asked.

"Nary a one."

"Good," Ian said. "I never know when it's safe to leave you alone. So tell me about this mystery—and about exactly how much contact you've had with the tall, dark stranger."

"An English stranger," Annie said, "with an accent and all."

Ian looked gloomy. "I don't suppose he was really old or really ugly?"

"Only a few years older than you," she said brightly. "And very handsome."

"Swell."

~ 20 ~

nnie laughed at Ian's glum expression. "He's here look-ing for a lost love," she said. "I'm pretty sure the woman he is looking for *is* in Stony Point, but I found that out when I was looking for answers to a totally different mystery."

Ian blinked. "Why are your mysteries always so complicated?"

"They're more interesting that way," Annie said. "But let me start at the beginning of each mystery, and I think it'll make more sense."

"OK," Ian said carefully. "Start with the one that in-volves the stranger."

"It's better if I start with the other mystery," Annie said. "Someone has been leaving little gifts all over town. They're lovely little cats made with a craft technique called needle felting."

"What's that? Is it like knitting?" Ian asked. Annie knew knitting was something Ian understood since Mary Beth had let out his secret some months before—Ian Butler could knit! He and his brother, Todd, had been taught by their mother when they were boys.

"It's a technique that uses wool roving, which is the fluffy stuff that yarn is made from," Annie said. "But you use a needle to tangle the fibers into a kind of felt. At any rate, the little cats are lovely. And they've appeared in the library, A Stitch in Time, the diner, the church, the post office, and my front porch."

"Your porch?" Ian echoed.

"Yes. Apparently the artist knew Gram," Annie said. "Anyway, the artist leaves thank-you cards with the gifts, and with a little help, we eventually recognized Candace Caine's handwriting."

"Should I know who that is?" Ian asked, looking more confused than ever.

"No, though it would certainly be helpful if you did," Annie said. "She's a children's picture-book author and illustrator who used to live in England but now lives in Stony Point. She apparently has changed her name, but I don't know what name she's going by. I thought it might be Nancy, but her handwriting doesn't look anything like Candice's, and Nancy doesn't really like kids."

"You know that this Candace Caine likes children?" Ian asked weakly. "How do you know that?"

"Well, I assume most picture-book authors *probably* like kids," Annie said. "But in this case, I know it for sure because Adam Smithfield *said* she does."

"And he is?"

"Her publisher and the tall, dark stranger," Annie said. "He's looking for her and seems to be in love with her. I'm not totally sure I believe him. I think I do, but I believed people in the past and then learned they were lying. Gram was always so much better at judging character. I tend to believe everyone."

"I know," Ian said, putting a hand over Annie's. "It's one of your more endearing and terrifying traits."

"Terrifying?"

"You must admit—it's gotten you into a lot of trouble in the past. I sometimes worry about you."

Annie nodded. That was true enough. "Anyway, Adam came to Stony Point looking for Candace, and now I'm pretty sure Candace really is here. But I don't know exactly where, or what name she is using. And I don't know if I should tell Adam what I do know."

"You and the tall, dark stranger are on a first-name basis?" Ian asked.

"He's in love with Candace," Annie reminded him. He didn't look all that comforted. "At any rate, Candace is the person who gave Boots to Gram."

Ian looked at her in shock. "Oh! I saw her."

Annie felt a surge of excitement. "You did?"

Ian nodded. "Arianna and I were going to the Friends of St. Francis to look for a pet. We weren't sure whether we wanted a dog or a cat." He chuckled. "In fact, Arianna wasn't convinced we needed a pet at all since we were both so busy. She thought that if we had a pet, it should be a cat since they're more independent, but I've always been a dog person. In the end, we decided to hold off." His smile faded a little with the memory.

"But you saw Gram?" Annie asked gently.

"Yes, with a little tiny woman," Ian said. "I know Betsy introduced us, but the poor woman looked like she was going to bolt and run. I don't know that I'd ever met anyone so shy."

Something about Ian's description tickled Annie's memory. "What was her name?" Annie asked.

Ian shook his head. "I honestly don't remember. I mostly remember how scared she looked."

"Did she seem scared of anyone in particular?" Annie asked.

He shook his head. "I remember wondering if she might be an agoraphobic, and thought maybe Betsy had coaxed her out into public, but I guess that wasn't it as I've seen her a few times since."

"Recently?" Annie asked.

"I'm not sure," he said. "She's easy to overlook, like she blends in with the world around her."

Annie nodded. Grace Emory had said something a lot like that about shy women going unnoticed. Annie wondered if Candace had always been so shy, or if Adam really had given her a good reason to be afraid. Was he more than the brokenhearted suitor that he appeared to be?

"So, now you're up to date on our two mysteries, that are really just one mystery. Candace Caine ran away from London and hid out here in Stony Point. She knew Gram. And now she's giving gifts to the community," Annie said. "Only I don't know who she is."

"Are you sure it's fair to track her down?" Ian said. "If that shy woman who was with Betsy is this Candace Caine, she really wouldn't want the attention of the whole community on her. I'm sure of that."

"No matter what I do, I'm affecting her life," Annie said. "If I let Adam give up and leave, how do I know that's what she'd want? If I tell him flat out that she's here and giving out cat sculptures, will that hurt her? I think all I can do is find her and ask her—if I can figure out who she is."

"Well, if you need my help, let me know," he said, and then he nodded toward the window. "In the meanwhile, it looks like it has stopped raining, so I need to go out and collect my luggage. Do you want to wait here?"

"No, I think I'll head home. I'm glad you're back. I've missed you. You're great to bounce ideas off."

After Annie had collected her wet clothes in a bag, she slipped her feet into her slightly squishy shoes and gave Tartan a last pat goodbye. Tartan wagged his tail for her, but Annie noticed he kept his eye on Ian the whole time.

"I'll return your shirt," Annie said, "and these pants."

"They belong to Todd's wife, Becky," Ian said. "I ended up with them after an unfortunate muddy-dog incident when they were visiting. I'm not certain she wants them back."

"Becky?" Annie said. "I thought her name was Elizabeth."

"It's actually Rebecca Elizabeth," Ian said. "Only family gets to call her Becky. Well, family, long-term friends, and whomever we forget and speak in front of." He laughed. "She thinks it's too cutesy, but I think she's doomed to be Becky forever in our minds."

Annie smiled. "I remember wishing my name was something more exotic or elegant when I was a girl. Alice and I even made up movie-star names for ourselves once."

Ian's face lit up with amusement and curiosity. "And what names were those?"

"I was Anastasia Louisa Spencer," Annie said, "and she was Desire Destiny Desmond."

Ian burst out laughing. "Alice didn't even like her last name?"

"She was really into alliteration," Annie said with a giggle.

"Well, thanks again for your help, Anastasia Louisa," Ian said. "Send my regards to Triple D."

"Oh, no," Annie said. "You better not let Alice hear you call her that. She'll never speak to either of us again!"

The sun was setting on the short drive back to Grey Gables. Annie knew how quickly sunset turned into night in Maine and hoped she made it inside before dark. She had been chilled enough for one day. As she drove, Annie went back and forth in her own mind about what she should do next. She had met two people who remembered Candace, but only vaguely. Mary Beth felt there was something familiar about the way Candace wrote her letter "I." Since she wasn't the only one involved in the search, she had to face the fact that it might not be up to her to put an end to it either.

After she pulled into her drive and climbed out of the Malibu, Annie heard someone shout her name. She turned to see someone walking up the driveway. Already the evening shadows made the figure hard to see, but Annie had easily recognized Alice's voice.

"You left without me," Alice scolded.

"I'm sorry," Annie said. "You weren't home when I got ready to go. I was too fidgety to wait."

"That's fine," Alice said. "I got a call from the husband of one of my Princessa jewelry clients. He'd forgotten his anniversary and was desperate for a necklace to give as a gift so his wife wouldn't know. I drove over to his office to let him pick from among my samples."

"Oh—sneaky," Annie said.

"It's all in the name of marital harmony," Alice said.

"Plus, I hate to turn down a sale. He ended up buying a necklace, ring, and earrings set."

"Sounds like your errand was more productive than mine," Annie said.

"You'll have to tell me all about it," Alice said, her eyes sweeping over Annie's outfit. "And tell me where you've been shopping."

"Come on in, and I'll tell you all about it," Annie said. "Have you had supper?"

Alice shook her head. "I was going to make a sandwich and soup after I talked to you."

"I have some great chowder I can warm up," Annie said. "It was delicious the first time, so I know it'll be even better now. We can have it with grilled-cheese sandwiches, if you don't mind putting the sandwiches together while I warm up the soup. You know how it is with chowder, you have to stir it constantly. How does that sound?"

"Marvelous."

As they walked through the door, Boots trotted over, though she quickly snubbed Annie after a sniff. "You'll be happy to know I'm done with dog duty," she told the cat.

"Oh, is Ian home?" Alice asked.

Annie nodded. "He came back just as Tartan and I were caught in that downpour. So he has now seen me looking like a drowned rat. He insisted I come inside and drip all over his floors. And then he insisted I change into dry clothes."

"That outfit is definitely a new look for you," Alice said. "It's nice to see you and Ian are so *comfortable* with each other.

"This is not a look I want to cultivate," Annie said. "It *is* cozy and a lot more comfortable than sodden linen and cotton. I guess if Ian could survive seeing me wringing wet, he probably wasn't all that horrified by the baggy, borrowed clothes." She held up the bag of wet clothes to prove her point. "I need to get the sweaters in the washer. The pants will have to go to the dry cleaners while I hope for the best. It's not like I shouldn't have known better than to wear linen while dog walking."

"So, did you find out anything interesting at the vet?" Alice asked as she idly watched Annie put the sweaters in the washer.

"Dr. Martin didn't have time to talk to me," Annie said. "Though she's supposed to call tonight, assuming I haven't already missed her call. Still, I did talk to Nancy Breaker."

Alice's eye roll matched the sarcasm in her voice. "Lucky you."

"Actually, I thought for a while that she might be the cat artist."

Alice laughed. "You're kidding—right?"

Annie closed the lid of the washer and turned the knob. "Consider it a moment of temporary insanity. I don't think it anymore. At the veterinary clinic, I discovered that she spent some time in England like Candace Caine. She clearly loves cats; Kate said she has four. She can do the kind of fine crochet that was on Mary Beth's cat's pillow."

"But can you seriously picture someone carrying a torch for Nancy for years?" Alice asked as she followed Annie back to the kitchen.

"People change," Annie said as she pulled open the

fridge door and began unloading the chowder and the makings for the sandwiches. "Nancy could have been a very different person when she was younger."

Alice took the sandwich makings and carried them to the counter. "But you don't think it's Nancy now?"

Annie sighed. "Not really. Not since I've talked to two people who actually saw Candace Caine when she helped Betsy pick out Boots. One was Ian and the other was Josephine Booth."

"You talked to people who actually know her? So now you know who she is?" Alice asked. "Way to bury the lead. You could have told me that *first*."

"No, I don't know who she is," Annie admitted as she poured the leftover chowder into a small pot and handed Alice a pan for the grilled cheese sandwiches. "Ian remembers her as an extremely shy woman, and he believes he's seen her around. Josephine said almost the exact same thing. And when I asked around at the library about a very shy frequent patron, every librarian had a different suggestion. You wouldn't believe the number of shy women in Stony Point."

"You know, I probably would have been on that list when I first came back after my divorce," Alice said. "I hadn't thought about it, but people could have thought I was shy or just unsociable. Sometimes life has a way of making you shut down to other people."

"But apparently Candace has kept that shyness all this time. At any rate, it totally takes Nancy out of the running. No one would describe her as shy." Suddenly, Annie's eyes widened. "Speaking of Nancy, she was going to send me a photo she'd taken of Grey Gables."

"She took a photo of your house?"

"She had a neighbor take a bunch, and she used one in a mock-up flyer for the tour of homes, so I could see how great Grey Gables would look on the brochure," Annie said, pausing to sniff the bubbling chowder. The sandwiches were sizzling in the pan on the next burner, and Annie's stomach growled in anticipation. "You have to give Nancy credit for going after what she wants."

"Sure," Alice said, and then she spoke hesitantly. "Still, I'm thinking I might let her put the carriage house on the tour. I could use some of the Divine Décor outdoor line in the yard, and you know I have it all over the house. It would be a good way of showing off the things I sell. Though I think the idea of putting a rose garden in the Town Square is stupid."

"Impractical anyway," Annie agreed. "I know Nancy will be happy if you join the tour. Apparently she hasn't gotten a lot of takers. She was almost subdued when she talked about it at the vet's, blaming herself for being pushy. I couldn't admit that I suspected she was right. Her approach certainly got Stella's feathers ruffled."

"Stella stays semi-ruffled most of the time," Alice said.

Annie laughed. She had to agree with that. "Please help me remember to check my email as soon as we finish eating. Apparently Nancy came back for a last picture of the house about the same time our mystery artist delivered my needle-felted cat."

"Your cat? You got a cat?"

Annie laughed lightly as they carried their dinners to the table. "I forgot just how much has happened since I saw you last. Yes, there was one on the porch this morning after I walked Tartan. And when I went to the post office to mail the hats to LeeAnn, I found out they'd gotten a cat too. I took pictures with my phone. I'll show you as soon as we're done eating." The two of them settled into some very focused eating.

"I didn't realize how hungry I was," Alice said at last when all the soup and sandwiches were gone. "Now, back to the mystery. Show me the kitties."

They walked to the entry where Annie had put the little box on a table when she'd come home from Ian's.

"Oh, it's Boots!" Alice said when she opened the box. "She's absolutely adorable. I half expect her to hop out and demand to be fed immediately."

Annie handed her the card. "When Mary Beth saw this, she said the 'I' looked familiar."

"Not to me," Alice said. "Though I can see that it's the same handwriting as in those picture books. Maybe she'll remember where she's seen it."

"That would be nice," Annie said as she showed Alice the photos of the cat from the post office.

"The workmanship on all of these is amazing," Alice said. "What did Norma think of it?"

"She actually smiled," Annie said. "In fact, she was cheerful the whole time I was there. She told me they don't deliver mail to anyone named Candace Caine in Stony Point. So other than the cat, she didn't have any useful news for me." As Annie spoke, she and Alice walked into the living room. Annie's laptop still sat on the coffee table where she'd used it earlier.

The women sat on the sofa, and Annie booted up the computer and brought up her email. Annie found Nancy's email nestled between an email assuring her she'd won millions in a lottery in another country and an email coaxing her to buy meds online. Annie clicked on Nancy's email and then on the attached photo.

As Nancy had warned, the photo was not well focused. Annie enlarged it, but the detail only became fuzzier. "Well, I can see this is Grey Gables," she said. "Can you tell if the little white box with the cat in it is on the porch?"

Alice leaned closer and squinted. "I think it is. And what's that at the side of the photo?"

Annie looked at the even more blurred area of the photo. At first, she didn't have a clue what she was seeing. It was a little like staring at one of the more unusual paintings at the Museum of Modern Art in New York City. Then she yelped. "It's a bicycle! You can see the back wheel and part of the person sitting on it."

Again Alice squinted. She nodded slowly. "I think you're right. But the photo is a mess."

"Still, someone was at Grey Gables on a bicycle," Annie said. "Do you think it could have been Candace, dropping off the box?"

"Maybe," Alice said. "Did Nancy mention seeing anyone on a bicycle at the house?"

Annie shook her head. "Of course, I didn't ask specifically about a bicycle. I see a lot of people on bicycles once the tourists arrive, but you hardly see anyone now. She might remember." Annie looked over at the table that held her phone and sighed. She wanted to know, but she'd had a long day and wasn't sure if she had the energy for Nancy.

Alice followed the look. "I can call her. I need to tell her that I'd like to put the carriage house on the tour anyway."

Annie slumped in relief. "Would you? She can be a little draining."

Alice patted Annie's arm as she fished her cellphone out of her pocket. She pointed at the open computer. "But you have to look up her number."

"Actually, I have her card. Just a second." Annie grabbed her project bag and rooted around in it until she found the business card that Nancy had given her at A Stitch in Time. She handed it over, and Alice made the call.

Annie could hear Nancy's voice blasting into the phone as Alice held it back a bit from her ear. Alice began by telling Nancy about her interest in having the carriage house on the tour. The shriek of happiness threatened to deafen them both. Alice let the river of words pour over her for a moment, making agreeable noises now and then until Nancy seemed to be winding down a little. "I have a question to ask you," Alice said finally.

This raised Nancy's volume again, and Annie could hear her clearly say, "Anything you need to know. Of course we haven't finalized …." She lost the rest of the meaning in the gush of words.

Alice waited the talkative woman out and then said, "Actually, it's about the photo you emailed to Annie, the one of Grey Gables."

This time the torrent was apologetic as Nancy assured Alice that she had taken no unauthorized photos of the carriage house.

"That's good," Alice said, talking over her. "We can schedule a time for photos when the carriage house looks good. But I wanted to ask you specifically about this photo of Grey Gables. I see there was someone on a bicycle in Annie's yard. Did you see who that was?"

No sound came from the phone. Then when Nancy spoke, she was too quiet for Annie to make out the words. "Oh, that's too bad," Alice said finally. "I was hoping you had. The bicycle was in the edge of the frame."

More quiet talking, and then Alice said, "You're probably right. It was probably a teenager. Thanks anyway, and let me know when you have more information on the tour." She paused as another excited flurry of words burst from the phone. "I will. Thanks again, Nancy. Good night!"

Alice blinked rapidly and slipped the phone into her pocket. "Whew, she certainly can talk."

"But she doesn't remember the bike?"

Alice shook her head. "I suspect she doesn't pay much attention to things not directly related to her interests. She seems a little single-minded that way. Still, it was worth the try." Alice looked up toward the clock on the fireplace mantel. "I need to go. I have tax stuff to work on. Do you have any other interesting discoveries to give me an excuse not to go work?"

"Do you want an excuse?" Annie asked.

"To avoid dealing with taxes?" Alice said. "You know it."

"Only that Adam said he was certain Candace would be involved with children somehow," Annie said. "But she definitely isn't doing any volunteering at the library. Josephine and the others would have known her if she was. And when

I considered Nancy a possibility, I asked Ellen Whitaker if Nancy ever volunteered with the children at the church, but she doesn't."

"Not a surprise," Alice said. "If she spent tons of time with children, she wouldn't recommend putting a rose garden out where they play. Was Adam really sure about the children?"

"He seemed very definite about it," Annie said.

"So maybe we need to think of other places someone might work with kids," Alice said. "Substitute teachers maybe. Or tutoring. Or maybe she helps over at the preschool?"

"Those are good places to check," Annie said.

"I'll see if I can think of any others," Alice said, "and tomorrow we can start making phone calls and see."

"What would we say on the phone call?" Annie asked. "Do you have someone who might sound a little British and is desperately shy but likes kids?"

"Something like that. We'll figure it out in the morning. Meanwhile, taxes beckon."

Annie walked Alice to the door, hoping they had better luck with the mystery in the morning.

～ 21 ～

nnie awoke early Friday morning from a strange dream. She'd been chasing a woman who rode a bicycle down Main Street. The woman had been pedaling so slowly that the bicycle wobbled, but Annie still couldn't catch up. Once or twice she'd gotten close enough to just touch the back of the woman's rain poncho, but each time, Annie's fingers just slid off the slick plastic of the poncho.

The dream was incredibly frustrating, and Annie hadn't wanted to fall back to sleep and find herself chasing the bicycle phantom again. Her head still felt a little slow and heavy as she shuffled to the kitchen and put on a pot of coffee. Boots rushed into the room, stuck her nose into her empty food dish, and began meowing in protest.

"Patience is a virtue," Annie told the cat as she poured a portion of cat kibble into the bowl. If Boots was impressed by Annie's wisdom, she showed no sign and simply stuck her nose into the bowl and began crunching.

Annie poured herself a cup of hot coffee and walked to the table near the window. She was sipping the coffee gratefully when the phone rang. Annie carried her coffee with her as she went to the phone. She wasn't ready to face a conversation without it.

"Hello?" she said, glad to hear that her voice didn't croak.

"Hi Mom, I hope I didn't wake you. Herb left early as he has a job interview and it's a bit of a drive to the company. I wanted to call before I have to get the twins off to school."

"That's OK; I'm up," Annie said. "Though I'm still getting coffee therapy." She carried the cordless phone back to the kitchen table. "How's everything?"

"Not great," LeeAnn said. "You were right, Mom. I really blew it with the whole job thing."

"How do you mean?"

"I sent a few resumés to Maine for Herb, before I realized how much we really belong here. I know you told me I shouldn't, but I guess I just had to do *something*. Well, one of the companies called here yesterday, and Herb answered the phone. He was surprised to hear the company had gotten his resumé. Surprised and not very happy."

"Oh, honey, I'm sorry."

LeeAnn sighed. "I thought if he found out about the resumés, he might think I was being pushy, maybe. I really hadn't expected it to be any worse than that, but he accused me of not trusting him to take care of our family. He said if I trusted him, I wouldn't be sneaking around and sending out resumés. He thought I wanted to move up here so I'd have you to fall back on if he never got another job. I tried to tell him it wasn't like that, and that we would only move if we had to for him to find work. That didn't exactly hit him right either. We ended up in a big fight."

"That must have been really upsetting," Annie said.

"We both lost our tempers," LeeAnn said, obviously on the verge of tears. "I know we both said things we didn't really mean. Before bed we exchanged apologies, but it still feels a little chilly and awkward around here. I hate that feeling of not being sure of each other."

"Some things take time to get better," Annie said.

"I know. I should have listened to you. This morning I told him that I'd sent the resumés right after he lost the job when I was feeling antsy to do something to help. I told him that once I had time to think about it, I didn't even want to move to Maine. You know me, Mom—whenever I hit a roadblock, I want to jump over it in the biggest possible leap. I think that's what this was."

"Did he believe you?" Annie asked.

"Maybe. I'm not sure," LeeAnn said. "The problem is that he knows I would love for us to be closer to you, so he could totally believe that I'd want the security of being near you when we had a big financial worry. I'm just not sure he believes just how much I love *our* home and *our* neighborhood and all my friends and projects *here*. The twins love their school. I messed up everything, and I don't even have a good reason for doing it."

"It's human nature to want to get away from a scary place," Annie said. "Herb's joblessness was and is scary for both of you. So you probably fixated on Maine as a safe place to run to. I'm glad you're seeing things a little more clearly now."

"A little late," LeeAnn moaned.

"But not too late," Annie said. "Just be honest with Herb and give the situation some time. You guys will come through this. He adores you and the kids. Something like this won't create anything you guys can't work through. Just remember that Herb is dealing with a lot right now too."

"I hope everything will be all right," LeeAnn said, her voice falling to a near whisper. "I love him so much. I know a lot of people think Herb is a little stiff and a workaholic, but he's the best man I've ever known. He's right up there with Daddy."

"Maybe you should tell him all that. He's a good guy," Annie agreed. "You guys balance each other. I really think you're going to be fine."

"Thanks, Mom," LeeAnn said. "Oh, I just heard some rustling from the kids. I need to go and get them some breakfast. I love you, Mom."

"I love you too, sweetheart," Annie said.

Annie stared out the kitchen window as she sipped from her coffee and fretted about LeeAnn and Herb. Her daughter could be both headstrong and impulsive, but Herb knew both of those things about LeeAnn and clearly loved her. She'd told LeeAnn that she was confident that things would work out—and mostly she was—but she knew relationships could be put under a fierce strain by situations like this.

She'd once read that most marital arguments were about money. She'd even had a few heated discussions with Wayne over money during their marriage, though their fights were few and far between. She just wished she could call Gram and talk to her about LeeAnn's situation now. She'd always had such good advice. Annie didn't feel qualified to step into the role of wise matriarch; she sure wished the family still had one.

Annie swallowed the last sip of her coffee and jumped as the phone rang again. Annie assumed her daughter had forgotten something she meant to say and was surprised when a whispering voice responded to her greeting.

"Stop looking for Candace Caine," the voice whispered. "Leave her alone."

Then the call ended before Annie could say anything. She stared at the phone. The call had happened so quickly, she wasn't even sure if the person whispering was a man or a woman. If it wasn't Candace herself, why would anyone else want Annie to stop looking?

While Annie was staring at the phone in her hand, Boots walked up to the table and began meowing. Annie looked down at the cat, and Boots immediately dashed over to her now empty food bowl. "Forget it," Annie said. "I'm not *that* distracted. I just fed you."

Boots meowed plaintively, and Annie shook her head. She was always impressed by the cat's acting skills. She stood and rinsed her coffee cup, while casting another longing look at the pot. She knew drinking two cups of coffee on an empty stomach was not a good idea. She should track down some breakfast.

She opened cupboards and peered in mournfully, and then she walked to the refrigerator and did the same thing. Nothing looked particularly tasty. *How is it that I keep going to the store, but I can still look into a half-full fridge and find nothing to eat?* she thought.

Closing the fridge, Annie pulled out a cookbook and began flipping through it, looking for muffin recipes. She might not be nearly the baker that Alice was, but she could certainly manage something tasty to go with a second cup of coffee.

She had just flipped past banana nut muffins (she had no bananas or nuts on hand), lemon poppy seed muffins (no lemon juice or poppy seeds) and cinnamon apple muffins (no applesauce), when she heard a knock at the front door. Annie looked down at her robe and slippers and moaned. There was something about not getting dressed the second she got out of bed that brought morning callers.

She was hurrying to the front door when she spotted Alice on the porch with a basket. Annie quickly pulled the door open. "Please, tell me you've come to rescue me with muffins!"

Alice laughed and held up the basket. "Zucchini chocolate chip muffins to be exact. I used dark chocolate chips, so we can pretend it's health food. All you have to supply is the coffee—I ran out."

"Sounds like my kind of health food," Annie said as she waved Alice into the house with a flourish. "I have hot coffee just waiting for a muffin accompaniment. How did you manage to run out of coffee? That's like Stella running out of yarn!"

"I'm trying to cut back," Alice said. "I didn't buy as much so I could ration it a bit. But all I managed to do was run out. How do people who don't drink coffee keep from walking into walls?"

"I don't know," Annie admitted as they reached the kitchen. She grabbed another mug and poured two cups of coffee. "I like a good cup of tea, but I didn't sleep well last night, and I definitely need coffee."

"You too?" Alice said. "I kept having this dream where the little needle-felted cats grew and grew. Then they came alive and ran amuck in Stony Point."

Annie smiled. "You get points for interesting. Mine was just about chasing a woman I assume was Candace around town while she road on the world's slowest bicycle. I woke up feeling incompetent—and tired."

The two women slid into the chairs at the table, and Alice folded back the tea towel that covered the muffins. "It sounds like we both could use some success in solving this mystery," Alice said. She reached into the pocket of her jacket and unfolded a sheet of paper. "I did a search online after I left you last night, and I have the names and phone numbers of every place I could find where people work with children. I figured we could split them up and make calls— after we eat breakfast."

Annie reached into the basket and pulled out a warm muffin. She took a bite and moaned at the tender cake and its slightly soft chips. The sweetness of the muffins contrasted perfectly with the slightly bitter chocolate. "This is wonderful."

Alice took a bite of her own. "Oh yeah! I can feel the antioxidants racing through my body. Health food is the only way to live."

They ate in rapt silence for a moment, and then Annie took a sip of coffee and set the rest of her muffin on her plate. "I got a very odd call about Candace Caine this morning. I couldn't really tell who the caller was, but he or she told me to leave Candace alone."

Alice's eyebrows raised. "Maybe it *was* Candace. Why couldn't you tell if it was a man or woman?"

Before Annie could begin describing the weird whispery voice, the phone rang. "I'm so popular today," Annie said as she picked up the phone.

It was Dr. Martin. "I'm sorry to call so early, Annie," she said. "I fully intended to call last night, but I had to go to a little home farm on the edge of town. One of their goats was having a difficult time birthing her first kid, and I was there for quite a while."

"That's perfectly all right," Annie said. "I hope the little goat was OK."

"Oh, it was twins, a little billy and a little doe," Dr. Martin said. "Everything came out just fine—if you will excuse the pun."

"I'm glad," Annie said. "I've always thought baby goats are adorable."

"Those two were, for sure," the vet agreed.

"I actually wanted to ask you about Boots," Annie said. "Do you remember who gave Boots to Gram? I know she came from the Friends of St. Francis."

"You know, Betsy did tell me that a very kind lady talked her into adding a cat to her life," Dr. Martin said. "I never met the woman, but Betsy clearly thought well of her. Of course, your grandmother tended to see the best in everyone, didn't she?"

"She did," Annie agreed, feeling a surge of disappointment that another possible clue hadn't panned out. "Gram was very special that way. Are you sure she didn't mention the name of the woman?"

"Oh dear," Dr. Martin said, "you do have a lot of faith in my memory. Now that I think of it, she might have. It seems like I have some kind of word association of her name and Christmas. Maybe it was Noelle? No, no, I'm sure that's not it. Maybe Holly?" She paused, and Annie could picture the vet's face in fixed concentration. "I'm sorry, Annie. I can't do better than that. It might have been Holly, but it might not either."

"That's all right," Annie said. "It's actually a help."

After she signed off, she looked into Alice's inquiring face. "She thinks Candace might be going by Holly, but she's not sure. She thought her name reminded her of Christmas somehow. She never actually saw her though."

"Oh well," Alice said. "At least we can try the Christmas name angle when we make our calls. And we'll start the calls as soon as you tell me every detail about your morning mystery call. Demanding phone calls must mean we're getting closer."

"It might," Annie said as she fetched the coffeepot and split the last of the coffee between them. She repeated the words of the message and described the whispery voice.

"Sounds spooky," Alice said. "I love spooky."

"It was a little disconcerting," Annie said, "but at least the person didn't make any threats. I don't really feel like it brought us any closer to an answer, however."

"Maybe this will," Alice said as she tapped the call sheet. They split the list of possible businesses and started making calls. Alice used her cellphone, and Annie used her landline. Annie let Alice go first, so she could pattern her calls after her more socially adept friend.

"Hello," Alice said, her voice cheerful. "I'm looking for a woman who I believe may work for you. She's very good with children, but quite shy with adults. Her name is something Christmasy like Holly, maybe. I heard such good things about her way with children."

Annie waited tensely as Alice listened to the person on the other end of the phone. "I see," she said. "Yes, I suppose the woman's name might be Lily. She's a short-ish woman in her forties? No? Oh, no, I'm sure that's too young to be the woman I'm looking for. Thanks so much for your time. I must have gotten the business name wrong."

She drew a thick line through the day care's name. "One down," she said, "and I'd rather not think about how many we have to go."

Alice and Annie worked doggedly down the list. Most of the people were very polite and seemed truly sorry that they didn't know anyone fitting the description. A few offered names that fit in some way, but clearly were too young or too old.

Finally Alice got a possible hit from a call to a children's theater group. "Yes, I would guess that Mary might be a Christmassy name," Alice said. "Is Mary in her forties? She is? And shy? Excellent. Could I possibly speak with her?"

Alice crossed her fingers on her left hand and waved it back and forth as she waited for Mary to come to the phone. "Hello, Mary? I'm looking for an old friend of a friend. Did you happen to know Betsy Holden in Stony Point?" Alice's shoulders sank. "No? Have you ever been to Stony Point? Oh, really, you moved up from Georgia last year? Well, if you ever do get a chance to visit Stony Point, I believe you may like it. I'm sorry for bothering you." Alice paused for a long moment as the woman talked. Finally she spoke, her voice rushed as if trying to slip into the conversation. "Those sound like wonderful plays. I'll check out the website and think about it. Yes, I'm sure the children are very talented.

Yes, well, I need to go. Right, thank you, Mary. Yes, thank you. Bye."

Alice dropped the phone on the table and leaned back in her chair. "If that woman is shy, I had trouble seeing it."

They returned to the list and managed to call every single place by noon. Candace Caine didn't appear to be associated with any of them. "Maybe Adam Smithfield was wrong," Alice said finally. "Maybe she isn't working with children anymore."

"Maybe," Annie said reluctantly. "He seemed so sure."

"Well, we definitely gave it the old college try," Alice said. "I've talked until I'm hoarse."

"We've run into so many dead ends," Annie said. "Maybe we're not meant to find Candace Caine. Maybe she deserves her privacy."

Alice began folding the tea towel back into the now-empty basket. "You'll figure out something," she said. "You always do. Hey, would you like to go to the church bazaar together tomorrow? I think we deserve a treat after all that hard work. And since the bazaar starts tomorrow, it's the perfect goodie. I just need to go finish up my taxes so I can mail them off. Though if I find out that I owe anything, I'm probably going to be too depressed to buy much."

"You keep such great records," Annie said. "I would seriously be surprised if you find out you owe anything. I wish I had everything so well organized. I'd be scared to death to do my own taxes."

"It's easier if you keep up all year long," Alice admitted. "So, are we on for the bazaar in the morning? I'll provide breakfast again."

"You didn't need the extra temptation," Annie said, "but I'll certainly not pass up a chance for more of your fantastic baking. I'll be happy to go to the bazaar with you."

After all, it would take her mind off how horribly they were failing with this mystery. How could one person be so hard to find?

～ 22 ～

After Alice left, Annie considered working on more bazaar toys. Working on a crochet project was normally very soothing when she felt keyed up, and she definitely felt as if she were in a total muddle. Many times, problems that seemed monumental grew much more manageable after a few rows on one of the simple baby blankets she'd made so many of. Annie smiled. She wished her high-energy daughter could settle down long enough to take up crochet. She might find it helped unravel the knots she'd tied herself into.

Annie tapped her foot as she hovered next to her project bag. She felt something tugging at her pant leg and looked down to find Boots slapping at her tapping foot. "I'm one to be thinking critical thoughts about LeeAnn's restlessness. I can't even stand still. I don't think I would be too successful at crocheting right now," she said. "You know, if you were a dog, we could just take a walk."

Boots looked up at her and meowed plaintively.

"Right—if I stay in the house, you're going to talk me into feeding you again. I guess I'll take a walk by myself." She took a light jacket off a peg by the door and headed outside. The recent rains had cooled the air, and there was more of the usual spring nip in the air. Annie zipped her jacket up high to keep the wind off her neck. With the chill, she definitely didn't want to brave the beach.

She crossed the street and stepped over the loose chain that stretched across the gravel road leading to the lighthouse. She didn't plan to make the climb all the way to the lighthouse, but the gravel road would give her some exercise without the annoyance of passing cars.

She'd barely started when she heard the honk of a car horn on the street behind her. She turned to look and recognized Adam Smithfield's rental car. Annie waved and was going to turn back to her walk when the driver's door opened and Adam got out. "May I speak to you?" he called.

"I was about to take a walk," Annie called back, not really wanting to deal with the moral ambiguity of how much to tell him about Candace.

"May I walk with you?" he asked.

Annie sighed. "Of course."

Adam unhooked the chain blocking off the road and pulled in, parking off the road on the other side of the two stone pillars. He got out and called, "Will it be OK for me to leave my car here?"

Annie nodded. "The road is chained because it's narrow and tends to be treacherous in storms. They don't want people using it to drive up to the lighthouse and end up on the rocks at the bottom of the cliff."

"That does sound dreadful," Adam said. "Do you have many accidents there?"

Annie shook her head. "But the ones we have tend to be fatal, so the chain is a good idea."

Adam hurried over to her side, and they began the walk

up the steep road. On one side, the road was bordered by woods that sloped gently upward, and on the other was the steep drop to the beach below. Washouts from the fierce New England storms had really made the road too narrow to be safe for vehicular traffic. Annie knew the Historical Society maintained the lighthouse, and she marveled at the nerve it must take to drive up to the lighthouse these days.

"Do you walk up here often?" Adam asked, slightly winded.

"Not really," Annie said. "As you can see, it's pretty steep, but I was feeling restless today. I probably won't walk all the way to the lighthouse. I have to meet my friend Alice for lunch in an hour." It was a little white lie, but she thought it was a good idea for him to think that someone would be expecting her soon.

Adam nodded. They walked silently for a few minutes, but Annie sensed Adam had something to say. Finally, he ran a hand through his hair, making it stand up in wild spikes. "I talked to the women at the library again," he said. "I was sure Candace must be involved with kids there somehow. The young woman in the children's section was very excited about their little cat sculpture and insisted I look at it. The handwriting on the card was Candace's. I would recognize it anywhere."

Annie nodded without speaking.

"When I mentioned that, she said she knew it already," he said. "She told me all about her discovery and your visit. Why didn't you tell me that you knew Candace was in Stony Point?"

"I did hint at it," Annie said.

"I've been going mad with worry and frustration. This isn't a game, Mrs. Dawson. What exactly do you know about Candace? Where is she?"

"I honestly don't know," Annie said. "I know she's here and has been here for quite a few years. She knew my grandmother. She gave her Boots. And she gave me one of those lovely little cat sculptures in Gram's honor. But I don't know what name she is using now. I truly don't know where she is." Annie held off on telling him she might be going by a name that might be associated with Christmas. That seemed too vague to be any help.

"That still doesn't tell me why you weren't honest with me," he said.

"Frankly, Adam, I don't know you," Annie told him, "and I don't really know what happened between you and Candace. I don't know why she's hiding from you, and I don't know if I'd be doing her any favors if I helped you find her. I don't know what she's afraid of."

He looked at her in stunned silence. "I would never hurt Candace."

"Then why is she hiding from you?" Annie asked. "What is she so afraid of?"

"What happened between Candace and me is private," he said. "Unlike Americans, I don't feel the need to broadcast every intimate detail of my life across a dozen social media websites. I believe private things should remain private."

"That's your right," Annie said calmly.

"But you won't help me."

"Only if I am certain that helping you doesn't mean

hurting someone else—someone who was clearly a good friend of my grandmother."

Adam stopped walking and he loomed over Annie, his voice low and tight. "Are you sure your interest is really Candace's welfare? I heard about your fondness for 'mysteries.' Maybe that's just another word for meddling in the private affairs of others. Maybe you're just nosy."

Annie stepped back a pace and shook her head. "I believe we're done talking."

She turned and started back down the road. Adam reached out and grabbed her arm. "Tell me where Candace is."

She stared down at his hand until he let go of her arm. Then she looked up at him. "I already told you. I honestly don't know. And if I did know, I wouldn't tell you without her express permission. You think I'm a busybody? Well, I'm beginning to think you might be a bully, Mr. Smithfield. And I am not going to point a bully toward a shy woman who has never done me any harm."

"You're making a mistake," he said intensely.

Annie smiled. "It wouldn't be the first time. But this time, if I err, I will err on the side of caution!"

She turned her back on him and continued down the road. Adam rushed by her, striding rapidly down the road, nearly slipping once or twice on the loose gravel. *Well,* she thought, *it's not a real mystery if I don't manage to make someone furious at me.*

When she reached the end of the road, she saw that Adam's car was gone. She was glad of that. She'd had enough of that conversation. *So much for a relaxing walk,* she thought as she crossed over into her yard.

She decided on yard work as another way of unwinding. The spring rains brought down a nearly endless supply of small sticks that would create problems later when it grew warm enough to begin mowing. Annie gathered sticks by the armloads and carried them back to the compost piles where she dumped her leaves in the fall. There was something cathartic about snapping the sticks into small pieces before tossing them into the bins.

She continued poking around in the yard, pursuing small projects until it grew dark, and she realized she was starving. She'd worked right through lunch, though when she remembered the whole basket of muffins she'd eaten with Alice, skipping lunch didn't really seem like a hardship. She went in to fix supper while Boots complained about being left alone for hours without food, or at least that's what Annie assumed all the aggressive meowing was about.

After her early supper, Annie still felt too keyed up to settle. She wished she could call Gram for a solid dose of gentle wisdom. Then she thought of someone she *could* talk to.

She hopped into her Malibu and drove to the church. She knew Reverend Wallace often worked late at his office on Fridays to prepare his Sunday sermons. She also knew he wasn't in favor of uncovering the mysterious artist, but the mystery wasn't the only thing weighing on her mind. Her worry over LeeAnn was exactly the kind of problem Reverend Wallace could help with.

She hurried into the church and headed for the office. Ellen looked up from her desk and smiled brightly at Annie. "You're becoming my most regular visitor," she said. "You just caught me. I was about to head home for the evening. What can I do for you?"

"This time I was hoping to speak with Reverend Wallace," Annie said. "Is he in?"

Ellen nodded. "Let me see if he's free." She picked up the phone and told the reverend that Annie had come to see him. "He says you're welcome to come in, if you don't mind him eating while you chat."

"I don't mind," Annie said, "but I don't want to interrupt his supper."

Ellen lowered her voice. "Actually he hates eating by himself. He would go home, but Mrs. Wallace has him on a diet. He's been eating lunch and Friday dinner at his desk ever since."

Annie thanked the young woman and headed into Reverend Wallace's office. The minister was only a little taller than Annie and a bit portly, though Annie wouldn't have considered him fat. He stood as she entered and smiled. "How nice to see you, Annie."

"I'm sorry to interrupt your dinner," Annie said.

He waved away the apology. "You're brightening up a very dull meal. My dear wife is dieting and feels it's something we can share. So, I'm brown-bagging veggy wraps and carrot sticks for lunch. And I have broiled chicken and more veggies for dinner. I believe I'm going to grow rabbit ears and whiskers any day now."

Annie's gaze swept over the desk and the remains of his dinner as she sat in the chair across from him. "I don't know too many rabbits who eat Oreos."

"My one vice," he admitted with a laugh. "So now you

know why I don't go home to eat when I can eat at my desk where I keep a stash. But I do limit it to three cookies a day. A bit of self-control nearly worthy of John the Baptist."

Annie laughed. "I certainly won't being doing any finger-pointing after eating chocolate chip muffins with Alice this morning."

"Ah—Alice is a truly heavenly baker," he said. "But I'm sure you came to chat with me about more than treats."

Annie nodded. "I'm worried about my daughter, LeeAnn. She and her husband have hit a rough patch, and I don't quite know what to say to her. Gram was always such a fountain of wisdom, and in situations like this, I really feel my own inadequacy."

"Betsy Holden was a singular person," Reverend Wallace said. "But in situations where your grown children are going through difficulties, the secret is to give them room to make their own choices, to be supportive, not to take sides, and to remind them of their still greater support from the Lord."

"Oh well—I seem to have failed at everything except being supportive," Annie said. "I told LeeAnn I thought she was doing the wrong thing, and I didn't even mention prayer, though I've been praying for them." Annie felt tears gathering, suddenly certain that she'd messed up everything!

— 23 —

"Don't beat yourself up over it," Reverend Wallace said. "If there is one thing I'm sure of about you, it's that you weren't trying to run your daughter's life. Overall, how strong would you say LeeAnn and Herb's marriage is?"

"Very strong," Annie said. "They complement each other well, and they clearly love one another and the children. Normally, they're very open and honest."

"And how strong would you say their relationship with God is?" he asked.

"Solid," Annie said. "It's one of the reasons I was so pleased when LeeAnn married Herb. He's quiet about his relationship with the Lord, but it shows in a million different ways."

"Then I'm certain they'll weather this rough spot," Reverend Wallace said. "Just as I'm sure you weathered a few with your husband. And I know Betsy weathered a few with Charles."

Annie blinked at that. She rarely pictured Gram and Grandpa as anything but blissfully happy together. She did know they had had one spat, after her grandfather had retired and they were cleaning out his office in the carriage house. As an adult, Annie knew that it was unrealistic to think of them as perfect, but it also felt strange to think of Betsy and Charles Holden as normal people, as well as her beloved grandparents. "Thank you, Reverend Wallace," she said. "You've given me a lot to think about."

He smiled. "And you've given me a pleasant dinner companion. Really, I know it's difficult, but try not to worry too much."

Annie thanked him again and left. When she reached her car, she dialed LeeAnn's number but only got her voice mail. "I just wanted to say that I love you, and I'm praying for y'all. I believe you're going to come through this just fine. Just don't forget to lean on the Lord, LeeAnn. You don't have to do everything on your own."

When she ended the call, she closed her eyes and said her own prayer for LeeAnn and her family. She felt a real sense of peace about the situation by the time she got into her car and headed home for a quiet evening.

As soon as she got home, she called Alice and asked her not to bring over muffins in the morning. "I'm feeling guilty about all the goodies," she said. "I'm going to end up with a figure like Boots."

Alice laughed. "I can't quite imagine that. OK, do you want to leave about midmorning for the bazaar?"

"That sounds good. I'll meet you at your house."

Saturday morning started late when Annie forgot to set her alarm, and she was grateful they'd changed their morning plans. Annie ate oatmeal for breakfast and felt very virtuous about not giving in to the urge to pull out her muffin recipes again.

Alice was ready to go by the time Annie walked over to her house. Annie looked at the lovely scarf Alice had tied over her hair, and she knew Alice was going to suggest they take the Mustang with the top down to enjoy the warm, bright day. "I'll look like a dust mop by the time we get to the church," Annie said. "I should go back and get a band so I can pull my hair up into a ponytail."

"I have a better solution," Alice said, and she pulled a second scarf from her purse. It looked as if it were splashed with different shades of blue watercolor.

Annie tied it over her fine blond hair. "OK, let the cyclone begin!"

Alice laughed. "It's not that breezy."

"That's because your hair just looks better and better when it's wind-tossed."

"You mean bigger and bigger," Alice said. "That's why we have scarves. They're like tie-down ropes to keep our hair from launching!"

As they drove to the church, their conversation drifted to horrible hairstyles they had known and worn. "You should have seen me at the prom," Alice said. "Between my heels and my hair, I towered over my date. Plus, I could barely walk in my shoes, much less dance. Not that it mattered; I think my hair terrified the poor guy. He barely got near me all night."

Annie laughed. "I wore my hair up in a chignon. I thought it was very elegant, though it had so much hairspray in it that it felt crispy."

"Oh, I know exactly the look," Alice said. "Crispy helmet head. It was the other big prom look back then. I went for electrified lion, but crispy helmet head is a classic too."

By the time they reached the church, Annie was glad of the scarf because it helped cover her ears as well as her hair. The wind generated by riding in the convertible was *cold*!

They found a parking space in the already crowded lot. Clearly the church bazaar was a very popular activity that particular Saturday. The church hall buzzed with conversation as Annie and Alice walked in. Tables had been lined up against the walls and another row of tables ran down the center of the room. This left wide, comfortable aisles for browsers—which was very helpful as there were a lot of browsers. Annie could see they were mostly women, but a scattering of men and kids looked at the tables of goods eagerly. Annie and Alice had barely made it clear of the knot of people at the door when a small group of women called out to Alice.

One of the women waved for Alice to come over. "We need to talk to our Divine Décor connection, stat!" the woman shouted.

Alice turned to Annie. "Do you mind? They're nurses from the hospital and really good customers. I promise to just be a few minutes, and then I'll catch up with you.

"That's just fine," Annie said. "Go. Make the connection. I'll start looking around. Of course, if I beat you to any of the really great things, you'll have no right to complain."

Alice laughed. "I'll try to be brave."

Annie began to slip through the crowd in the room, thinking absently that with this many people, they should raise some good money for the food pantry. As she looked around, Annie's eyes fell on a lone figure flipping through the pages of an old book at one of the tables tucked in the far corner.

Annie remembered the woman from A Stitch in Time. It was the shy lady who had known Gram. What was her name? Suddenly it hit her. Ivy. The woman was named Ivy, like the Christmas carol *The Holly and the Ivy*. With a soft gasp, Annie realized she was looking at Candace Caine.

It all fit. Candace Caine was shy but knew Gram well, and Ivy had certainly shown a close familiarity with Gram at their first meeting. She was short, though almost painfully thin. Still, Kate had mentioned that she seemed to have lost a lot of weight. She might have been plump once. And she'd written something on a card for Mary Beth. Annie thought for a moment and then remembered—her email address and possibly her name. That could be why the "I" in Annie's note looked so familiar to Mary Beth. Had Annie finally found the answer to the mystery? She started slowly across the room.

Ivy looked up as Annie reached her table.

"Hello, Ivy. Could I speak to you just for a moment? There's something I really need to ask you."

Ivy looked at her silently for a moment, and Annie watched the play of emotions across the woman's face. She wondered if Ivy would just tell her to go away, but finally the thin woman simply nodded.

Annie stepped closer and leaned toward Ivy slightly, speaking very quietly. "You're Candace Caine, aren't you?"

Ivy sighed and smiled sadly. "I haven't been Candace Caine—except when composing books—in years. It's been long enough that it feels like a name that belongs to someone else."

"And you made those beautiful cats that have appeared around town?" Annie said.

Ivy nodded. "I love needle felting. I use it in some of my

book illustrations. I did one book with a little needle-felted cat, and it just seemed to want to pop out of the pages. He was a copy of a cat I once had, so I made him as a three-dimensional piece. After that, I made more and more little cats. They make me happy."

"Ebenezer," Annie said. "The first cat you made was Ebenezer."

Ivy looked at her in surprise. "How did you know the name of my cat? I know people talk about you being something of an amateur sleuth, but that's amazing."

"Actually, Adam Smithfield told me the name of the cat."

Ivy's face clouded. "I'd heard he was in town. I even saw him from a distance. He was walking up the steps to Maplehurst Inn. I nearly fell off my bike, I was so shocked. He hasn't changed at all. Not like me."

"He seems desperate to find you," Annie said.

"Yes, he's certainly put enough money into it," Ivy said. "It's been so many years. I really expected him to let it go long before now."

"You won't talk to him?" Annie asked.

"There's no point in it," Ivy said. "He'll look for a while longer, but eventually he'll go back to England and to his family there. He's married, you know. There's really no excuse for him to chase all over the world after *me*. His poor wife."

"Oh." Annie hadn't expected that. "Did he get married after you left him?"

Ivy shook her head and closed the book in her hand with a soft snap. She laid it back on the table and ran her hand gently across the worn leather cover. "He was married all along. Not that I knew. Not that he told me." She looked up at Annie and smiled sadly. "I was very young then. Not so much in years as in experience. Still, I was *not* the sort of girl who got involved with married men. I really wasn't. And Adam and I never ... well, we never did anything physical. But I fell in love with him."

"And you left when you found out he was married," Annie guessed.

Ivy nodded. "Of course. I couldn't do anything else. As betrayed as I felt, I knew my heart well enough to know I couldn't be around him. Eventually I would have forgiven him, and then I would have started making excuses to myself for why I should be involved with him." She smiled sadly again. "I really never expected him to care when I left."

"Are you sure he's still married?" Annie asked.

Ivy shook her head. "I haven't checked up on him in years. I did at first when I learned he was looking for me. I imagined he had divorced his wife so he could find me and marry me. But every time I made inquiries, Adam was still married. Finally, I decided it wasn't healthy to keep checking up on him."

Annie nodded. It sounded like Ivy was being sensible. But if Adam was married and intended to stay married, why was he looking for Ivy? "He told me that you were a lost love," Annie said. "Why would he lie about it? Was he ever cruel to you?"

Ivy shook her head. "I know I seem the sort who would meekly put up with abuse, but I am not. I respect myself more than that. No, Adam was always kind and not just to me; I never saw him behave unkindly to anyone. I wouldn't have left him my dear Ebenezer if I thought he had a cruel streak."

"He was more than a little short with me yesterday," Annie said.

Ivy raised her eyebrows questioningly, and Annie told her about meeting Adam during her walk. "Maybe he's growing tired of the hunt and will go back to London soon," Ivy said.

"Maybe," Annie said, "but he certainly seems determined."

A small group of women moved in on the table of old books and Ivy looked at them uneasily. "I really should be going," she said softly.

"Ivy," Annie said, dropping her voice to match Ivy's soft murmur. "I'd really like to talk more. Not just about Adam, but also about the cats."

"This isn't a good place," Ivy said.

"Would you have lunch with me?" Annie asked. "You could come to Grey Gables, or we could eat at the diner."

"I haven't been eating out much lately," Ivy said. "But I would love to come by Grey Gables for a cup of tea. It would be good to see Boots again."

"I'm sure she'd like to see you, too."

Ivy nodded, shifting her weight nervously as another group joined them at the table. "Perhaps this afternoon," she said finally, "but now I really must go."

Annie watched the smaller woman dart through the crowd like a minnow in a stream. Annie hoped Ivy would come to Grey Gables to talk with her. She now knew who had been leaving the little cats around town. She knew who Candace Caine had become, but she felt a lot of questions were still unanswered. Why had Ivy decided to give away all the little cats now? And why would Adam be looking for her if he was a married man?

Annie was still staring absently into the crowd when Alice popped up in front of her. "Wow, you sure look a million miles away," Alice said.

"Actually, I was just trying to sort out one more piece of the mystery puzzle," Annie said.

"You found another clue?" Alice demanded. "How come all the clue-finding on this mystery happens when I'm not around?"

"I happened to see Ivy Beckett," Annie said. "Do you know her?"

Alice nodded. "I think I met her once. She's really quiet." Then Alice froze and her eyes widened. "Do you think ...?"

"Actually, I know," Annie said. "Ivy Becket is Candace Caine. What I don't know is why Adam is looking for her."

"They aren't old loves?"

"Only in the sense that Ivy was once in love with him— and he was married. Ivy thinks he still might be married."

"Well, I would love to say married men don't fall for other women," Alice said, "but ...."

"I think there's more to it," Annie said, "but I know Adam is not going to explain it to me after our frosty encounter yesterday."

"And Ivy doesn't know why Adam is here?"

"She doesn't seem to," Annie said. "She said she would come over this afternoon for a cup of tea. Maybe I can find out enough answers to make sense of all this then."

"Maybe," Alice agreed, and then she grinned. "In the

meanwhile, come and tell me what you think about this hand-painted lampshade I found. I think it would look fantastic in my bedroom, but I need a second opinion."

"With your decorating sense, you want my opinion?" Annie asked.

"Opinion, encouragement, whatever," Alice said. "It's a little pricey. I need a nudge."

"So—your taxes apparently didn't cut too deep, did they?" Annie joked, following Alice through the crowd to a table of hand-painted items. The shade was lovely. Alice needed very little encouragement before money changed hands, and she was walking around carefully carrying the shade in a bag.

Suddenly Alice froze and turned around. "All those places we called," she said. "Does Ivy work with kids somewhere?"

Annie nodded. "Right here at church in the Sunday school. I remembered that Ellen mentioned it when I was trying to find out if Nancy worked in the Sunday school. She had a photo of everyone in the department. That's when she told me that Peggy had volunteered for a while because Ivy was sick."

"Oh, so you already knew that when we made all those calls?"

"Actually, yes," Annie said. "I just hadn't realized that Ivy could be Candace. She's definitely not plump."

"That's true," Alice said. "Oh well. Making all the calls gave us an excuse to eat an entire basket of muffins. That was fun in a bloated way."

Annie laughed. "If we had too much fun like that, I'd be the one described as plump!"

Annie put the whole mystery completely out of her mind and concentrated on enjoying the bazaar. She picked up some darling doll clothes that she knew would fit one of Joanna's dolls. And she bought a clever wooden coat hook in the shape of a ship that she thought John would enjoy having in his room.

Alice bought a beautiful, small, grapevine basket. "When you make as many muffins as I do," she said, "you can never have too many baskets. I actually have a cross-stitch pattern for grapevines and leaves. I'll make a cloth to line this basket with that design. It'll be great."

When they'd seen everything, they headed toward the door with their new treasures. Just as they got outside, they ran into Ian. "Mayor!" Alice said. "It's nice to have you home again. Stony Point nearly fell to pieces without you."

Ian laughed. "Somehow I doubt that."

"Maybe it was just Annie who nearly fell to pieces," Alice said, her eyes sparkling with mischief.

Annie just shook her head. "Well, I have to admit, Tartan tried to wear me down to a nub once or twice. I honestly tried to walk him until he wore out."

"Oh no," Ian said.

"Actually I came close one day when I took him for a walk on the beach," Annie said. "He slept all the way back to your house."

"And bounced like a jumping bean out of the car when you arrived—right?" Ian asked.

"Yes," Annie admitted. "It was a short-lived victory, but I still savored it."

"Sounds like Tartan had a marvelous time while I was

away," Ian said. "No wonder he's a little glum. He probably misses you, Annie."

"Oh, the *dog* misses you, Annie" Alice said. "Maybe you should go over there."

"Great idea," Ian said. "How about tomorrow after church? I can make a Sunday dinner and impress you with my cooking. And maybe Tartan will cheer up."

"That sounds like fun," Annie said, "and I'd hate to think of Tartan pining away."

"Yeah, cause he's such a melancholy little thing," Alice said.

Annie gave her the look that always worked on LeeAnn when she was a teenager. Alice appeared to be amused and merely grinned at Annie.

"Excellent," Ian said. "I'll see you tomorrow at church. And now I need to go support the bazaar by buying things."

When Annie got home, she left the front door open so the warm spring breeze could come in. She hurried upstairs to put the things she'd bought safely away from prying paws in the closet of the guest room where she usually stored gifts. She left her own closet door open a crack too often to make it a Boots-proof area. Then she retrieved her laptop from the living room. If Ivy was coming by, she wanted the room to look friendly and inviting, not cluttered.

Before she left the computer in her bedroom, she started it up to check her email. She was surprised and pleased to find an email from LeeAnn. The email itself was short, "Things still thawing here, but it's looking good. Herb's old boss called and apparently they really can't get along without him. So the job hunt is over for now. Plus he got a raise! Thanks for everything, Mom. I thought you'd like to see your two little pirates." Annie clicked the attachments link, and a photo filled the screen. It showed Joanna and John dueling with long cardboard tube "swords." They were both dressed in bits of pirate costume. John even grasped a "hook" in the hand that wasn't holding the sword. The twins had their heads turned to face the camera, big grins pasted across their faces. Annie saw then where John had lost a tooth.

She smiled and typed a quick message back to LeeAnn. "Tell John he looks very rakish!"

She was heading back down the stairs when she heard a soft knock at the door. Annie spied Ivy standing on her front porch. She opened the door and smiled. "I'm so glad to see you, Ivy. Please, come in, and I'll put on the kettle for tea."

"I've been wanting to come inside since the day I left the little cat," Ivy said. "I spent so many happy hours in this house."

"So have I," Annie said. "Gram made this place the most love-filled house I've ever seen."

"She certainly did," Ivy agreed as she followed Annie down the hall to the kitchen. Annie put the kettle on to boil, and gestured toward the table. "Do make yourself comfortable. Can I offer you anything to eat? I think I have some cookies, or I could make you a sandwich if you're hungry."

"No, no thank you," Ivy said. "Tea will be fine."

Annie poured the water when it neared boiling, just as Boots marched into the kitchen. "Oh, Boots!" Ivy cried. She slipped out of her chair and scooped the cat up into her arms. Boots purred loudly and rubbed her head against Ivy's chin. "I don't think she's changed a bit since I saw her last."

"She certainly seems to have a long memory," Annie said. "I can see that she likes you a lot—and misses you."

Ivy buried her face in the cat's soft thick fur. "She reminds me so much of Betsy too." Ivy looked at Annie. "I miss your grandmother terribly."

"So do I," Annie said.

Finally, Ivy placed the cat gently on the floor, and the two women sipped their tea in companionable silence, each lost in thoughts and memories. Ivy began reminiscing about specific things Betsy had done or said that she remembered. Annie chimed in with her own memories of her grandmother. With each shared memory, Annie could feel a bond forming between herself and the quiet woman across from her.

"Mary Beth told me that Gram had tried to talk you into joining the Hook and Needle Club," Annie said when they finally began to run out of memories to pour out.

"Betsy was always trying to get me to mix with people more," Ivy said. "She worried that I was lonely."

"Were you?" Annie said.

"Not really," Ivy said. "I really have never needed to be around lots of people. If I have one good friend, I'm content. When I get in groups, I feel overwhelmed. It's been that way my whole life. Your grandmother was that good friend for me."

"Are you lonely now that she's gone?"

"Sometimes," Ivy admitted. "But my circumstances have changed now too. I'm not certain I would be a particularly good friend for anyone."

"Why do you say that?" Annie asked. "I admit I don't know you, but in the little time we've shared, you seem like someone who would be a wonderful friend."

Ivy smiled, and the smile was so incredibly sad that it almost made Annie weep. "There's something about me that you don't know."

"What's that?" Annie asked.

Before Ivy could answer, they both heard a loud rattling knock on the front screen door. "Oh, I'm sorry," Annie said. "That's probably Alice. Do you mind if I ask her in?"

"Of course not," Ivy said as she stood up. "I remember Alice. Your grandmother often told me stories about the two of you."

"Oh no," Annie said as they walked down the hall toward the front door. "I hope they were good stories."

"They were certainly *interesting* stories," Ivy said, her voice full of good humor.

Just at that moment, they both recognized who stood on the other side of the front screen door, and he recognized them. Adam Smithfield stared open-mouthed at Ivy as she stood frozen in the hallway. He didn't wait for Annie to reach the screen door, but merely opened it himself. "Candace?" he said, his voice full of amazement. "I can't believe it's you. It is you, isn't it?"

"Oh, Adam," she said sadly. "Why are you here?"

"Because the possibility of never seeing you again was unthinkable."

~ 24 ~

nnie stood between Adam and Ivy. She wasn't sure what to do. Should she try to make him leave? As she looked into the man's stricken face, she wasn't entirely certain if she could make him do anything.

"Ivy?" Annie said.

Ivy pulled her gaze away from Adam to look at Annie. Seeing the concern on Annie's face, Ivy smiled weakly. "It's all right, Annie. I suppose I wasn't being very realistic, thinking I could avoid this. Thinking Adam would leave me in peace."

Adam reacted to her words with a wince. "Is that what you want? You want me to just leave?"

Ivy looked back at him, her gaze steady. The shy woman Annie had seen earlier was gone now. "Would you?"

"I don't think I can."

"You should go home, Adam," she said quietly. "Go home to your wife."

"If that's what you want," Adam said, "but let me explain."

"Explain a wife?" Ivy said, raising her eyebrows. "I may never have been married, but I believe I don't need wives explained to me. I understand the concept, though I'm not certain you do."

"I deserve that," Adam said, "but I'm still asking for a chance to explain."

Ivy sighed. "All right, all right! We can talk here, if Annie doesn't mind." She turned to Annie, and for a moment Annie saw a flash of self-doubt in the woman's eyes. "Would you stay with me? I'd rather not have this discussion alone with Adam."

Adam looked horrified. "You have to know I would never hurt you."

"That ship has sailed, Adam," she said, her gaze snapping back to him. "You could have hit me with your fist and not caused as much hurt as I've had from you. Can you begin to fathom the pain of finding out the person you love is married and simply didn't tell you?"

"Love?" Adam said softly. "Do you love me, Candace?"

"Candace Caine is dead," Ivy said. "She died the day she heard about your wife. She's just a pen name now—a ghost I use to publish books."

The two of them stared at each other silently. Annie took the opportunity to ask quietly, "Would you like to come into the living room? Surely it would be better not to have this conversation in the hall."

Adam looked at her in surprise as if he'd forgotten that Annie, too, was in the room. He nodded mutely. Annie led them into the living room, and Ivy sat perched on the edge of a chair while Adam sat on the sofa as close as he could come to her.

"All right," Ivy said. "Try to explain yourself, and I won't interrupt." She folded her hands into her lap and looked at him expectantly. The pose reminded Annie of a child sitting politely for a particularly dull lecture.

Adam ran a hand through his hair, his eyes darting

around the room as if looking for inspiration. Finally he said, "When I was a boy, there were two small publishing houses in London that struggled. My parents owned the one that my father's parents had begun. The other house belonged to the Chethworth family. They had one child, just as my parents did. Their child was a daughter—Honoria."

"Your wife," Ivy said.

"Eventually." Adam smiled grimly. "Our marriage was championed heavily by both families. It would unite two companies into one strong unit, without either house leaving the families that founded them. It was the sensible, dutiful thing to do."

He stopped for a moment. His eyes dropped to his own folded hands. "Honoria was beautiful. Tall. Icy in many ways. But we got along well enough, considering."

"Considering?" Ivy repeated.

He smiled sadly. "Honoria didn't really care for me—or for any man. She made her preferences known to me before the wedding. It wasn't a surprise. I didn't care. I had no real interest in the traditional marriage and family. Our parents were unhappy when no children came along, but they resigned themselves to it, I suppose."

"That sounds lonely," Annie said.

He turned his eyes to her. "Not as much as you'd think. Honoria and I were friends. She's pleasant company. And all our energy went into our work. It worked for the first years, but then her interests veered away from publishing. She became interested in fashion. Our company began a fashion magazine. Honoria moved to Paris, a city she adored. I stayed in London. We saw one another yearly for a business meeting."

He turned to Ivy. "I wasn't looking for anything different. I thought my life was fine. Then I met you. In my life, everything was planned, orderly, and rigid. You were completely different and utterly brilliant. I was fascinated."

Ivy didn't speak, but Annie could see her eyes swimming in tears.

"Still, I didn't mean for our relationship to be more than friends," Adam said. "I told myself that was all it was. I told myself you were like my lively little sister. I told myself that my protective feelings for you were brotherly, and my desire to be with you constantly was friendship."

"You could have told me," she said softly.

"Then I would have been lying to both of us," Adam said. "I was falling in love with you. I knew better than to suggest anything illicit. Even I am not such a total idiot that I couldn't see you would never be open to becoming someone's mistress. So I began looking into the legalities of divorcing Honoria. I knew it wouldn't be a hostile divorce. She has no possessive feelings toward me. Then one day, I called you, and you didn't answer. I came to your flat and all I found was Ebenezer and a note saying only that you were leaving, and that I should not follow."

"And," she said, "you stayed married after I left."

He nodded. "At first, I simply didn't have the time to move forward with the complexities of unraveling the marriage from the business. All my energy went into finding you. I was certain that would take only days, maybe weeks." He looked up at her. "I underestimated just how much you hated me—how much energy you'd put into running from me."

He paused. Annie wondered if he was waiting for Ivy to say she didn't hate him. Annie knew she didn't, but Ivy sat silently and waited for him to finish.

"Then when I got back to London, I was angry," he said. "I was angry with you for not giving me a chance to speak. I threw myself back into the business and told myself that it wasn't worth the effort to divorce over a relationship that never really existed."

That last remark made Ivy wince, but Adam just went on. "Then your books began coming in again. Of course we published them. You were just as brilliant, and the books took on a sense of melancholy that struck a chord with awards committees. Each time a new package came, I took up the search again at the city where the package was sent. Each fruitless new search drained away more and more of my hope, but I couldn't stop. Then you sent me a letter."

She nodded, but still didn't speak.

"I couldn't quit after holding a note in your own handwriting, even though the contents offered me no hope of reconciliation," he said. "I hired detectives, but they gave up. So I came to America. I came here. I found you."

"To what purpose?" Ivy asked. "You're still a married man."

He shook his head. "You've not kept up so well lately. Honoria died two years ago in a plane crash on the way to fashion week in Milan. There were so many more well-known people on the plane that no one paid much attention to Honoria. I hadn't seen her in several years. She'd even stopped attending the yearly business meeting, but I was still sad. We had been good friends, after all, if nothing more."

"I'm sorry," Ivy said. "I didn't know."

"Even if Honoria were still alive, she would have granted me the divorce. We had no claim on one another beyond the company." He laughed without humor. "If we had been Catholics, we might even have been able to get the marriage annulled since it was never consummated. It was a business deal entered into to make our parents happy—it was never a marriage."

Ivy shook her head. "So what do you want now?"

"I love you," he said. "We've lost so many years. I'm willing to stay in America. That easily can be arranged. We can start slow if you want. I'll buy you flowers and take you to the theater. We can walk on the beach. Whatever you want."

She shook her head. "You should go back to London."

"No," he said. "Not now that I've found you again. I'm not walking away."

"Not even if it's what I want?" she asked.

"How can it be what you want?" he said.

"Because I don't have time for you, Adam," she said. "I don't have time for us. I don't have time for anything. Look at me. Don't you see how I've changed?"

"You look beautiful to me."

"Look closer. Does it look like I'm dying?" she asked, her voice nearly a whisper. "Because I am. And your money, your stubbornness—they can't change that." She stood up and walked out of the room as Adam and Annie stared after her.

~ 25 ~

nnie heard the screen door close with a quiet bump and knew Ivy must have left the house. She looked at Adam, but had no idea what to say to him. She had found the answer to the mystery. She knew why Ivy was giving gifts to the people and places she loved in Stony Point. It was a quiet gesture from a dying woman. She knew why Ivy had left Adam years before, and why Adam had come to Stony Point. She knew the answer to her mystery, and the knowing broke her heart. She couldn't imagine how it felt to Adam.

He finally stood without speaking and turned to the door.

"Will you be all right?" Annie asked him.

He shook his head, not turning around. "No, I don't believe I will." His voice cracked. Then he walked out of the room, and Annie heard the front screen door again. Annie sat back down, unsure of what she should do. After a few minutes, Boots jumped into her lap, startling her. She tearfully wrapped her arms around the cat, and they sat together as shadows slipped across the room.

The next morning, Annie briefly considered pulling the covers over her head and skipping church. She'd slept poorly, having lain awake until the early hours of the morning. She still felt confused and very sad. She dressed carefully, choosing a blue floral dress that swished around her legs pleasantly. She hoped a little extra makeup would help hide the dark circles under her eyes.

When she got to the church, she saw Ian waiting at the top of the wide church steps. His face broke into a smile at the sight of her, and Annie remembered that she was supposed to go to his house for dinner. She wondered briefly if she could beg off. She smiled back at Ian, though her smile felt a bit stiff. "Annie, what's wrong?" he asked, clearly alarmed. "Is it LeeAnn or the kids?"

"No, they're fine." She patted his arm absently. "I had some trouble sleeping last night. I really don't want to talk about it right now. Would that be all right?"

He nodded and took her hand tucking it into his arm as they walked into the church. Annie paid little attention as Ian led her to a pew and took a seat beside her. She looked around the room and blinked as she spotted Ivy sitting near the front of the sanctuary in a beautifully tailored rose linen dress. Annie didn't think Ivy looked ill, though her thinness did give her an air of fragility.

Ian followed her gaze and then looked surprised. He nodded toward Ivy. "That's the woman you asked me about— the one who was Betsy's friend. She's looking a bit thin, but that's definitely her."

Annie nodded. "I know. She's the one who has been making the little cats."

"You solved the mystery."

She nodded.

"But you wish you hadn't?"

"No. I'm glad I did," she said, leaning her head onto his

shoulder. "I just wish it had a happier ending." Realizing how that might look, Annie straightened up, turning to look at Ian.

Ian spoke gently, quietly. "Not every story does."

She smiled at him. "No, I suppose not."

She turned her gaze back toward Ivy and spotted Adam striding up the aisle to Ivy's pew. Ivy looked up at him, clearly surprised and not particularly pleased.

Annie saw Adam speak to her. Ivy shook her head at him. He slid into the pew beside her and took her hand. He spoke again, his face intent. Annie watched a look of wonder pass over her face.

As Reverend Wallace took his place at the podium for announcements, Adam and Ivy turned their gazes toward the front. Annie noticed that Ivy let Adam hold her hand. She stole glances at them now and then during the service, seeing that he never let it go.

Somehow Annie knew that love had won out. And she knew in her heart of hearts that Adam and Ivy would somehow fill whatever time God gave them with all of the laughter and tears and heartache and joy that only love could bring. Annie glanced at the strong, good man beside her, knowing that she, too, had been running from love for a long time.

After the service, Ian walked out with Annie. "You know," he said. "If you're not feeling up to it, we can postpone our Sunday dinner plans. Tartan will understand."

Annie smiled at that. "I can't think of anyone I would rather be with today than you and Tartan."

Ian smiled widely. "And I can't think of anyone I'd

rather be with any time than you. When I was driving back from New York, I was feeling a little lost and very alone. Then I saw you in my yard, dripping wet."

"Thanks for that memory," Annie said ruefully.

"You looked so horrified," Ian said, laughing, "and there was Tartan shaking more water onto you. I realized then that I didn't need to feel so alone after all."

"I imagine it's hard to be lonely with Tartan around," Annie said, half-kidding.

Ian smiled. Folding her hand over his arm again, they walked down the church steps. "That's part of the reason I'm not lonely any more, but not the biggest—or the best—part."

And with that, he walked her to her car in the beautiful spring sunshine.